I0582886

CLEAR FOR ACTION!

by Stephen W. Meader

THE BLACK BUCCANEER	THE FISH HAWK'S NEST
RED HORSE HILL	SPARKPLUG OF THE HORNETS
AWAY TO SEA	THE BUCKBOARD STRANGER
LUMBERJACK	GUNS FOR THE SARATOGA
WHO RIDES IN THE DARK?	SABRE PILOT
T-MODEL TOMMY	EVERGLADES ADVENTURE
BOY WITH A PACK	THE COMMODORE'S CUP
CLEAR FOR ACTION!	THE VOYAGE OF THE JAVELIN
BLUEBERRY MOUNTAIN	WILD PONY ISLAND
SHADOW IN THE PINES	BUFFALO AND BEAVER
THE SEA SNAKE	SNOW ON BLUEBERRY MOUNTAIN
THE LONG TRAINS ROLL	PHANTOM OF THE BLOCKADE
JONATHAN GOES WEST	THE MUDDY ROAD TO GLORY
BEHIND THE RANGES	STRANGER ON BIG HICKORY
RIVER OF THE WOLVES	A BLOW FOR LIBERTY
CEDAR'S BOY	TOPSAIL ISLAND TREASURE
WHALER 'ROUND THE HORN	KEEP 'EM ROLLING
BULLDOZER	LONESOME END
THE CAPE MAY PACKET	

THE ROPE SPLASHED WITHIN A YARD OF THE
EXHAUSTED MAN

CLEAR FOR ACTION!

by

STEPHEN W. MEADER

Illustrated by
Frank Beaudouin

© 1940 HARCOURT BRACE AND COMPANY, INC.
© 1968 STEPHEN W. MEADER
© 2006 SOUTHERN SKIES LLC

All rights reserved

ISBN 978-1-931177- 48-1 cloth
ISBN 978-1-931177- 49-8 paperback

SOUTHERN SKIES

LITTLE ROCK, ARKANSAS

www.southernskies.com

Dedication

The republication of this book is dedicated with love to Clinton Parham Edwin Atchley---scholar, researcher ,professor, raconteur, wit, great brother--- by Jerry Atchley.

ILLUSTRATIONS

CLEAR FOR ACTION!

CHAPTER I

COMING over a rise in the road, Jeff saw the little, white-painted schoolhouse, nestled among the pines on his right. Off to the left was a blue arm of the sea. And straight ahead, above the trees, he could catch a glimpse of a slim church steeple pointing to the sky.

It was noon recess, he judged, for the school-yard was full of small boys and girls at play among the rocks and brambles. Some of them stopped their romping and stared at him, big-eyed, as he strode past.

"Looky, Noah!" he heard one youngster whisper excitedly. "That's Jeff Robbins an' he's goin' to sea. Betcha he's got pistols an' ever'thing in that bag he's a-carryin'."

Jeff gripped the tied end of the bag more tightly and hunched it higher on his shoulder. The little boy's surmise was flattering if a long way from the truth. It was only three years since Jeff himself had played in that schoolyard and he remembered the romantic thrill of looking at a genuine deep-water sailor.

"When's the *Abigail* sail?" one of the bolder lads asked him.

"Tonight's tide if the wind's right," he answered with the gruff indifference he thought proper to his age and calling. And whistling a careless air he stalked on in the direction of the village.

Actually he felt far from indifferent. He was about to start on his first real voyage, and excitement ran high in his veins. Ever since Captain

Josiah Preble had signed him on as a foremast hand, two weeks before, Jeff had had to pinch himself occasionally to make sure all this was true. From the time when he was five years old and first rowed a dory, he had looked forward impatiently to this day. It might have come sooner if the Embargo and Nonintercourse Acts hadn't kept so many ships in harbor. As it was, he knew he was lucky to get a berth aboard the *Abigail*. Captain Preble had found a little trouble in rounding up a crew for the old schooner. Some of the more experienced seamen in the neighborhood were working at other jobs and one or two had prudently decided to stay ashore when they heard that the voyage was to the West Indies.

The energetic housewives of Shinnequid Cove had taken advantage of the mild March sunshine and were busy with their spring cleaning. Windows were open in the square white houses Jeff passed, as he walked down the main street of the village. Patchwork quilts were out to air and braided rugs were being beaten in dooryards.

At one gate in a white picket-fence the young

sailor hesitated a moment, stealing a glance at the big, comfortable-looking house. He wondered if Patience Deering was at home but he felt some shyness about going in to ask. More likely, he told himself, she was out driving with her father. The squire took a lot of pride in his matched team of blacks.

Jeff passed the general store, the tavern, and the tarry-smelling ship-chandler's shop at the foot of the hill. A pair of oxen stood sleepily on the planking of the dock, jaws moving in slow rhythm as they chewed their cuds. Behind them Jeff saw a long wagon-frame loaded with lumber. Four or five men were lifting the boards and stacking them on the deck of the schooner that lay moored alongside the wharf.

The *Abigail* was not a thing of beauty, even to Jeff's prejudiced eyes. Her lines were stubby and broad in the beam. Like most of the old coasting-schooners she was built for seaworthiness and cargo capacity rather than for grace or speed. Her deck house and weatherbeaten black sides needed paint, and her sails, furled on the booms, were dingy gray.

As the boy stood there staring at his ship, a man strolled toward him. "H' are ye, lad?" the stranger greeted him. "I cal'late ye're the new hand, ain't ye?"

Jeff nodded and looked at the man curiously. He was a grizzled old shellback in sea-boots and jacket, a battered officer's cap tilted on the back of his head. His face was brown and seamed, and his blue eyes held a frosty twinkle.

"Cap'n told me about ye," he explained. "I'm Ephraim Jones, first mate. Ever been to sea afore?"

"No," Jeff answered. "I'm plenty used to boats, though. Maybe you know my dad—he keeps the lighthouse on Tombstone Reef."

"Ye don't say! Many's the time I've been glad to pick up that yeller beam, comin' in from a v'yage. You his helper?"

"Part o' the time," said Jeff. "Mostly I fish and run a line o' lobster-pots."

"Ain't much of a livin' in lobsterin', is there?"

"Well, on a good day I can pick up a shilling

or two. The taverns down Portsmouth way pay a penny apiece for prime lobsters. I sail 'em down myself twice a week."

"Hmm—well, ye ought to make a seaman, soon's ye learn the ropes. Ain't feared o' the British, be ye?"

Jeff laughed. "No," he said, "I haven't thought much about the British, anyhow. Too glad to get a chance on a ship."

"They ain't likely to meddle with us this trip. We aim to hug shore all the way down. Still, there's sailors 'round here that ain't got your grit. They'd ruther be landlubbers than run a chance o' bein' 'pressed."

He shifted his quid and shot a stream of tobacco juice into the tide. "How old be ye?" he asked.

"Seventeen last month," Jeff replied, standing up a little straighter. "Folks sometimes take me for older."

"Ain't so tall," said the mate, critically, "but ye got a good broad pair o' shoulders. Shouldn't be s'prised if ye'd make a reefer one o' these days."

Their conversation was interrupted just then by the arrival of Captain Josiah Preble. He was a spry, white-bearded little man with a salty roll in his gait.

Giving Jeff a brief nod he turned on the mate with a nervous gesture of his gnarled hands. "What in 'tarnation ye doin', gabbin' here, Eph?" he asked querulously. "Don't ye see there's a westerly wind makin'? How 'bout that deck-load o' planks? How 'bout them galley stores?"

"Now, Josiah," Jones soothed him, "the stores has been under hatches since forenoon, an' I been keepin' a weather eye on the lumber. There— see? They're carryin' the last planks aboard right now. Tide won't turn anyhow till 'most sunset. What ye want to git so upsot about?"

"All right," the captain fidgeted. "I'm anxious to git to sea, that's all. Round up the crew an' have 'em stow their dunnage. I'll want all hands where I can see 'em. Mebbe we won't wait fer the tide, with this breeze."

Jones shrugged his shoulders and winked at Jeff. "Hop up to the tavern, sonny," he advised, "an' pass the word fer the *Abigail's* men. Look alive, now. Leave yer sea-bag right here."

The boy crossed the wharf at a trot and climbed the muddy hill to the inn. Because the day was warm the door stood open, and he could see a dozen figures clustered along the bar. As his boots crunched on the sanded floor he heard voices raised in argument.

A big, black-haired fellow with a red face thumped his pewter mug on the dark, stained wood. "I'd like to see any dirty lobsterback try to 'press *me!*" he shouted. "I'm a citizen o' the State o' Massachusetts an' the United States of America! I got my rights an' I'll stick up fer 'em."

One of the other drinkers chuckled. "Them's brave words, Jonas," he said. "Wait till one o' them cruisers spits a round-shot 'crost our bows. I'll be waitin' to hear ye speak up to 'em."

The swashbuckler swallowed his ale with a scowl, and when the general laughter had subsided, Jeff gave his news.

"Cap'n wants all hands down to the *Abigail* right off," he announced.

There was a grumble from one or two of the crew, but they picked up their chests and bundles and started straggling toward the schooner. It was a motley array of sailormen that gathered on the dock a few minutes later. A few of them Jeff knew—Maine coast fishermen like himself. One was a lad about his own age, who had been on a couple of coasting voyages. He was a big, hulking, good-natured youngster named Amos Gilman. There were several sober-faced, elderly men, forced back to sea by the hard times, and two or three Shinnequid ne'er-do-wells and tavern-loungers. Out of the whole ship's complement of twelve people, Jeff saw only two that he would class as able seamen. They were Jonas Beale, the big, black-browed fellow who had voiced his defiance of the British press-gangs, and Nate Winslow, a rangy, quiet-faced downeaster who hailed from Wiscasset.

"All right, men," the little captain barked.

"Git for'ard an' stow yer dunnage. Lively there! An' try to act like ye'd seen a ship afore!"

Jeff took his turn at the forecastle ladder, scrambling down into the narrow, V-shaped space and looking around him with some disappointment. It seemed impossible that ten men could sleep in such quarters with any comfort. But already the older hands were dumping their belongings in the best bunks, aft, and he saw that if he didn't stir himself he would get last choice. Hastily he laid a hand on the edge of one of the upper berths and was about to swing his bag into it, when Jonas Beale squeezed past him without ceremony. "Lubbers lay for'ard," the big sailor grinned. "This here's a berth fer a seaman."

Somewhat chagrined, Jeff found himself and Amos Gilman jostled into the low-beamed peak of the forecastle, where there was barely room to stand between the bunks. Amos laughed. "G-g-guess we're 'lected, Jeff," he said. "I'll take p-p-port an' you take starboard."

At its widest part, the crew's sleeping place

was not more than ten feet across, and its length was about eighteen feet. There were three double tiers of bunks on a side. Down the middle stretched a narrow trestle table, with benches that pushed under it when not in use. Two small portholes let in a little daylight, and a dingy whale-oil lamp swung from the deck-beams above.

"Shucks," said Gilman, "this ain't bad at all. I was in a b-b-brig last fall that didn't have but five-foot bunks. Had to s-s-squizzle up like an inch-worm to sleep in 'em."

Half an hour later they were lined up on deck for the picking of watches. The captain had first choice and took Beale. Jones immediately countered by selecting Winslow. After that the discussion grew violent. Preble swore his mate was cheating him out of all the decent hands, and Jones made belittling remarks about the quality of the material left for him.

"Listen to 'em!" chuckled Amos, who had been chosen in the mate's watch along with Jeff. "S-s-squabblin' jest like a pair of old women at a rummage sale."

When it was over, the captain clawed at his chin-whiskers and spat over the side. "Good 'nough," he grunted. "Now all hands git sail on her. Homer, have 'em shake out them jibs an' stand by to cast off moorin's. You, Beale, git the lashin's off the mains'l an' the rest of ye man the halyards. I'll take the wheel."

In the bustle that ensued, Jeff was too much occupied to notice what went on ashore. Only when he heard his name called did he turn from the jib-sheets to see a pretty girl standing on the wharf. Somewhat red in the face he spoke to the mate.

"Mr. Jones," he said, "someone's here to say good-by. Could you spare me a minute?"

"Spare ye?" snapped the old salt. "Fur's I can see ye ain't wuth a hoot an' a holler here. Go on an' hug yer gal, but make it sharp!"

Rubbing the rope-tar off his hands on his breeches, Jeff sprang across to the dock. "Gee, Patience," he grinned shyly, "I never expected to see *you* down here!"

Patience Deering tossed her brown curls. "I saw you this noon," she replied. "Walked right past the front gate, and didn't even stop to see if I was home! A nice way to act!"

Her blue eyes met his teasingly, then dropped. "I guess you'll—be gone a long time, won't you, Jeff?" she asked.

"Can't tell." He tried to sound matter-of-fact. "With good luck and a fair wind we might be home in two months."

"Father thinks the voyage is foolish, right now," she said soberly. "With all this talk of war, he's afraid you may run into trouble. Promise me you'll take care of yourself, Jeff."

He promised, with a light heart. "What's in that bundle you've got?" he asked.

The girl blushed and looked down at the toe of a slipper that peeped from under the billowing skirt of her red dress.

"It isn't much," she said. "Just something I made for you. Here—take it!"

She thrust the parcel into his hands and kissed him so quickly he hardly knew it had happened.

Then she was running up the hill while he stood gawking after her, open-mouthed.

A chorus of laughter and cat-calls from the deck broke in upon his daze. "Can't ye see she's gone?" bellowed the mate raucously. "Git back aboard here 'fore I wake ye up with a rope's end!"

Jeff ran below to hide the parcel in his sea-bag, then hastened forward. The jibs were already hoisted and the mainsail was going up to the chant of the men at the halyards. Jones tossed the mooring-cables aboard and leaped nimbly across the widening stretch of water between the dock and the schooner's side.

Ashore, a little group of relatives and onlookers cheered and waved their kerchiefs as the *Abigail's* bow swung out to catch the offshore breeze.

Captain Preble turned the helm over to one of the seamen and hopped about, yelping his orders through cupped hands. In a moment the schooner was standing out into the cove. Her sails were drawing nicely, and Jeff could see that she was making headway against the inflowing tide.

Slowly the village dropped astern and the shore began to slip past. Flat, brown marsh where the ducks went up with a flurry of wings at their approach. Bleak, gray ledges, crowned with bayberry and wild-rose thickets. Headlands shaggy with spruce, and rolling pastures where sheep were grazing.

When they cleared the mouth of the cove the schooner footed faster. Jeff took his station on the port side, holding to the foreshrouds and looking intently into the northeast. As they passed Shinnequid Head he got a view of the lighthouse. It was a stubby white tower, half a mile out to sea, perched on the bare ridge of Tombstone Reef. White water broke hungrily along the lonely rock at its base. It was too far for any daylight signal to have been made, but Jeff imagined his father up there in the tower, watching the *Abigail* through his spyglass. He snatched off his dark jacket and waved it two or three times against the lighter background of the foresail. As if in answer, a beam of the setting sun caught one of the lamp surfaces and flashed a blinding reflection across the miles of tossing water.

Amos Gilman's heavy hand came down on Jeff's shoulder. "We're off to sea, my lad!" his deep voice boomed. "How's it f-f-feel?"

CHAPTER II

IN THE excitement of sailing, Jeff had forgotten all about food. But at sunset, when four bells were struck, he heard the call to supper with enthusiasm. He remembered then that he had eaten nothing since breakfast.

The starboard watch had already had their meal and were on deck when Jeff and his mates went down the companionway. At the foot of the ladder stood the lean, sad-faced mulatto cook, holding a steaming kettle.

"Mmm!" Amos Gilman murmured. "Chowder, by ding!"

There was a rush for spoons and pannikins, and as the crew crowded around him the cook ladled out a generous portion for each man.

With a hard slab of sea-biscuit in his left hand and an iron spoon in his right, Jeff settled down at the table to enjoy his meal. It was good chowder. Plenty of haddock, potatoes and onions had gone into it. If ship's fare was going to be as tempting as this, he decided life at sea would be a lot of fun.

Jeff had the second dogwatch below, and as soon as supper was over he went to his berth. It was the first opportunity he had had to look at Patience Deering's gift. Lying on his side, to screen the parcel from the eyes of the forecastle, he undid the strings and opened the paper.

The first thing he came to was a knitted sleeveless vest of warm wool. There was a little note pinned to it. "You can wear this under your oilskins on cold, stormy nights," he read. Then, inside the folds of the garment, he found another package—two dozen crisp, brown cookies, knobby with walnut meats.

"Gee!" he whispered. "And she made 'em herself!"

Almost reverently he took a bite of one of the cookies. A yard away in his own bunk, Amos must have heard the crunch of teeth. "Hey!" the big youngster stammered. "Robbins—y-y-you got somethin' to eat there? Give us a taste!"

In ten minutes the cookies had all been devoured.

.   .   .   .

Jeff had a short nap before the watch was changed at eight bells. When he came on deck the *Abigail* was slipping along southward with a quartering offshore breeze. In the darkness it was impossible to see the shoreline, and even the schooner's sails and rigging were vague masses, merging with the murky sky overhead. The only light abovedecks was the shrouded beam from the binnacle lantern. In its dim, yellow glow Nate Winslow's strong hands could be seen, shifting on the spokes of the wheel.

For the first two hours Jeff sat in the lee of the piled lumber, lashed under a tarpaulin amidships. On that course and in that light wind the schooner almost sailed herself, and the men had little to do. About the middle of the watch, however, Mr. Jones called the boy forward to relieve the lookout in the bows.

"Ain't much chance o' sightin' another sail," he told him, "but keep an eye peeled to loo'ard jest the same. What ye want to watch fer is shore lights. We'd ought to pick up the Isles o' Shoals 'fore midnight. No drowsin', now!"

Jeff took up his position beside the coiled hawser, as far forward as he could get. The schooner's bluff bows lifted and dipped sluggishly to the quartering seas and under her forefoot the water gurgled past. Once, twice, the ship's bell clanged the half hours. Stiff and cramped, the young seaman shifted from one foot to the other. His eyes ached from staring into the empty dark. He had been too much in small boats to be bothered by the schooner's pitching and rolling, and the monotonous heave of the deck made him sleepy rather than seasick. But still he kept his lookout, first off to seaward under the bellying foot of the jib, then in the direction of the hidden land.

It was nearly seven bells when he rubbed his eyes and leaned forward. He thought he had seen a glimmer on the water. "Light, Mr. Jones!" he yelled.

"Where away?"

"Two points on the starboard bow."

"Good 'nough. Hold her as she is, Winslow."

So that, Jeff mused, was the little light on the Isles of Shoals. The northerly islands must be nearly abeam now, and he was leaving his last familiar landmark. The *Abigail* was logging about four or five knots, he thought, in that light breeze. If the wind held, daylight would find them nearly abreast of Cape Ann. Half an hour later he went below with the watch and tumbled into his bunk, half asleep before he had kicked off his boots.

This business of sleep was one of the greatest

difficulties Jeff encountered in adjusting himself to sea routine. Roused out at the end of his four hours, he was yawning and stumbling as he climbed to the deck.

Amos Gilman laughed at him. "What's the matter, farmer? Can't you wake up till the roosters start crowin'?" he asked.

Jeff was too drowsy to answer. He shivered in the chill of the early dawn and buttoned his jacket tighter. The darkness was beginning to gray in the east. As the horizon cleared, one of the hands hailed from forward. "Sail, ho—on the port beam!"

Mr. Jones and the watch clustered along the rail, looking off to sea. They could make out the sail now, hull-down to leeward.

"Ain't a man-o'-war, that's sure," the mate announced, peering through the spyglass. "Ketch rig, looks like, an' the tack she's on ought to bring her pretty close astern."

For the next hour the *Abigail's* crew watched the other craft as their courses slowly converged. She was running close-hauled under full sail and making such good headway that it was soon apparent she would cross their bows.

When the ketch had come up within a cable's length she fell off on a parallel course to the schooner's. They could see a big man standing aft by the stumpy mizzen-mast and hear his shout coming across the water.

"Ahoy! What schooner's that?"

"*Abigail* o' Shinnequid. Who are you?" Jones bellowed in rejoinder.

"*Lady Ann*, Gloucester. Fisherman. You aim to cross the bay in daylight?"

"Why not—with a favorin' breeze?"

"Suit yerself, then. But there's a couple o' king's ships cruisin' off Boston. Might take a fancy to some o' yer crew."

The skipper of the fishing ketch stamped back to the wheel, turning his back on the *Abigail* to show the interview was over.

"Hmm," said Mr. Jones, rubbing his bristly chin. "Mebbe I'd better have a word with the cap'n."

He went below, and when he returned a few

minutes later the schooner's helm was put over. With Jeff and two of his messmates hauling on the main sheet, she headed to windward and followed in the wake of the *Lady Ann.*

An hour after sunrise they sighted Eastern Point and shortly dropped anchor off Ten Pound Island in Gloucester harbor. Captain Preble took two of the crew and went ashore in the schooner's single small-boat, while the mate kept the rest busy aboard. As much of the deck as was not covered with lumber had to be scrubbed down and the few pieces of brasswork polished. Jeff was given a paint-bucket and put to work touching up the weatherbeaten after-house.

He had time, between strokes of the brush, to view the waterfront of the famous fishing port. There was evidence of the trouble caused by British cruisers in the number of craft tied up along the piers. The masts of schooners, yawls and ketches fringed the waterfront like a forest. In the roadstead a few larger craft, brigs and full-rigged merchant ships, lay at anchor, their cordage sagging from disuse. Jeff knew from hearsay that the same conditions prevailed in Salem and Boston, New York and Philadelphia, Baltimore and Charleston. Thanks to Mr. Madison and his timid policies, American shipping was almost at a standstill in that spring of 1812.

Perhaps this voyage of old Captain Preble's was foolhardy, but the boy felt a thrill of pride in the fact that Maine men were still willing to risk danger on the sea. He worked at his painting through the morning and early afternoon, and when the skipper returned, about three o'clock, his task was done.

The weather was still fair and the wind held true from the west. "Give all hands a rest," Captain Preble told the mate. "We won't make sail till sundown."

Dusk was falling over the sea when they cleared the harbor and bore off on a long southeast slant to pass Cape Cod. Double lookouts were kept, on the eight to twelve watch, but they made the first half of the journey across Massachusetts Bay without sighting a sail or a vessel's lights. Then the wind began to drop! At midnight, when Jeff went below, the canvas was barely drawing and there was a damp feel in the air. The boy knew the signs. "We aren't likely to be picked up now," he told Amos with a yawn, as they crawled into their berths. "It'll be thick fog in another hour."

Sure enough, when the watch came on deck again the cordage dripped and the schooner was muffled in a gray blanket of moisture. Such air as was stirring came from the east now. It was a slow beat to windward, sailing by dead reckoning.

All morning the fog hung thick. At four bells in the afternoon watch the wind freshened a little and the fog lifted enough to show them a low, sandy shoreline a few miles to starboard.

Nate Winslow nodded approvingly. "The Old Man knows what he's doin'," he remarked. "Hit the tip o' the Cape square on the nose, fog or no fog."

For the rest of that day they made a long reach southward, keeping the dunes in sight and heaving the lead at regular intervals. Another misty morning found them feeling their way through Nantucket Sound. They had a brief glimpse of Martha's Vineyard at noon and then left land behind to cross the choppy stretch of sea off the mouth of Long Island Sound.

The captain had heard in Gloucester that more British cruisers might be expected around Block Island. For that reason the *Abigail* bore well to seaward and made all sail to pass Montauk before daylight.

They skirted the Long Island shore next day without mishap and once more used the darkness to cross the hazardous entrance of the port of New York. Jeff was on lookout duty in the second dog watch, when they left Fire Island astern. The breeze was southerly now, but with her main and foresail sheeted home, the schooner could be brought close enough to the wind to make for Sandy Hook on a single long tack.

There was still a faint light on the sea to westward when Jeff sighted a speck of sail standing toward them out of the lower bay. Mr. Jones studied the stranger through the glass till darkness swallowed her, and was still in doubt.

"Had the look o' one o' them fast sloops-o'-war," he mumbled. "I'm thankful there's no moon, or she could overhaul us quick enough. Hey! Up for'ard there—trim that jib. She's spillin' wind!"

Whatever the other ship was, they saw no more of her that night, and daybreak gave them something else to think of. It was raining and blowing gustily from the east, so that they had to begin beating offshore almost as soon as they sighted the Jersey Highlands.

The constant tacking made heavy work for the watch on deck, but there were intervals when it was possible to talk. Some time in the forenoon Nate Winslow pointed into the gray smother to leeward. "Right down there a way," he told Jeff, "is a part o' the coast every skipper likes to steer clear of."

"Rocks?" asked the Maine boy.

"No rocks off Jersey," Winslow said. "Nothin' but sand, an' no special bad shoals at that. But many a fine ship has piled up there, an' never a soul of her crew left to tell of it."

He went on to give Jeff an account of the Barnegat wreckers who set false lights to lure unwary shipmasters into the breakers. "There's cruel trades aplenty," he ended, "but none blacker than the murder done by wreckers."

Jeff shivered. "You mean they kill all hands on board?" he asked.

"There's no way o' sayin', for sure," said the big sailor. "Why? Because dead men tell no tales."

Jeff stayed near Nate Winslow whenever he was able. It was a lesson in seamanship just to watch his brown, muscular hands splice a rope or bend a bowline. He had sailed before the mast from the time he was twelve and won a mate's license while he was still in his 'teens. But for the decline in shipping caused by the embargoes, he might have been in command of his own vessel.

All this Jeff learned gradually, for the tall down-easter never talked much at a time. Once he chuckled quietly when he heard the captain and mate having one of their squabbles on the afterdeck.

"To hear 'em jaw each other," he said, "ye'd think there was mutiny aboard. Wouldn't one o' them British Navy cap'ns be scandalized, the way a Yankee ship is run? Matter o' fact, we ain't so strong on their kind o' discipline, but we manage to get things done."

He was silent for a while and Jeff thought he had finished. But as soon as the schooner had gone about and the main sheet was taut on the new tack he turned to the boy with a frown.

"I know somethin' about their Navy discipline," he growled. "Two years I spent in a blasted big seventy-four-gun ship o' the line. I've got the marks o' the cat still on my back."

"You—you enlisted?"

The Wiscasset man tipped back his head in a sudden, savage laugh. "Yeah," he answered without humor. "That's what the press-gang called it."

The weather cleared that night but the breeze

hung between east and south and the *Abigail* was still working to windward. It was another twenty-four hours before they fetched the Delaware Capes. Halfway across to Henlopen the wind died and fog shut down.

Captain Preble cursed shrilly and danced up and down beside the wheel. "The tide's runnin' into the bay!" he wailed. "Driftin' like this we'll be halfway up to Philadelphia 'fore it turns. Git out the boat, Ephraim, an' start towin'."

The watch below was turned out and the boat put over the side. With eight men at the oars and Mr. Jones steering, they stretched a cable tight from the schooner's bow. Then began hours of dull, back-breaking work. Jeff could pull with any man aboard, but in the dripping fog, with the dead weight of the ship dragging astern, there was little fun in rowing.

If they made progress there was no way to tell it. Even the schooner, two hundred feet away, was so shrouded in mist that they could barely see her idly drooping sails. Some of the boat's crew—the tavern loungers—got blisters on their hands in the first hour, and shirked at the oars.

Jeff and Amos occupied the same thwart. They talked a little at first, then settled down in silence to endure the long strain of rowing. Suddenly there was an exclamation from somewhere forward in the boat. "Listen!"

The muffled boom of a cannon came rolling through the fog. And then, almost on top of them, they heard an excited shout. "Hey—boat, ahoy! Look out below!"

CHAPTER III

So close was the cry of warning that every rower stopped in the midst of his pull and stared upward. Out of the gray mist crept a ghostly bowsprit, followed by the massive cutwater of a big ship. Right over the boat's bow stood the carved and painted figurehead.

"Back water!" roared Ephraim Jones. "Lay on it or she'll swamp us!"

With a desperate lunge the oars caught the

water again and they sheered off barely in time. Slowly the towering oaken side moved past, almost in reach of the oars. Looking aloft Jeff could see an open gun-port, and above it the surprised faces of seamen at the rail. The great topsails and t'gallants were lost in the writhing mist.

"What firin' was that we heard?" asked the mate.

"That come from His Majesty's Frigate *Cormorant,* thirty-eight guns," answered one of the ship's crew elaborately. "She'll be along just in time to gobble up that hooker o' yourn. Not a mile astern of us when the fog settled down. We wouldn't heave to an' be searched like she wanted."

The tide ran fast between the capes and in a moment or two the vessel had drifted past. Below her broad cabin ports a name was gilded—"MAGNOLIA, PHILADELPHIA."

"One o' Girard's ships," the mate muttered. "She'll git away, too. Trouble never happens to rich folks."

"What in tarnation ye loafin' for?" squalled the captain from the deck of the *Abigail*.

"Jest passin' the time o' day with ol' Steve Girard," Mr. Jones answered sarcastically. "Come, lads—give way! Lay to it, now. We got to snake this tub out o' the way 'fore the frigate tosses another round-shot over!"

They needed no urging. Jeff could still hear the dull echo of the first report ringing in his head. He bent his back and wrenched the heavy oar through the water with all his might. The cable drew taut once more and the schooner crawled forward on her sluggish course.

Straining till the thole-pins creaked, even the malingerers were working now. None of them had any desire to run afoul of a man-o'-war and be forced into the service of the king. At his side, Jeff could hear Amos Gilman panting out his bitter thoughts.

"Gol-durn—n-n-nosey British—must figger —they own the—hull blame ocean!"

There was no let-up in that frantic rowing for half an hour. Then the mate held up his hand.

"Ye kin ease off for a spell," he said. "We must ha' towed the ol' scow a mile, an' the other feller's gone past by now."

After a brief rest they rowed for another hour in desultory fashion. Then Captain Preble called them back aboard. "Startin' to feel a breath o' wind," he announced. "Sails are drawin' an' I reckon we kin keep steerageway on her."

The breeze freshened little by little and the fog began to blow away. By sunset they were well past Cape Henlopen and bowling southward down the coast. The British man-o'-war must have passed astern of them in the mist and run on up the bay with the tide. At any rate, a careful search of the clearing horizon failed to show any glimpse of a sail.

By nightfall the *Abigail* was wallowing along in a choppy sea off the Maryland shore. During the evening watch Jeff tried to get Nate Winslow to tell him more about his impressment in the English Navy. The boy's imagination had been stirred by their narrow escape in the fog, and he wondered if all the tales he had heard were true.

But the lanky sailor was not in a talkative mood. "I was in a brig out o' Salem fer the Spice Islands," he said. "We come through a typhoon in the Indian Ocean an' started our seams. Had to run into Malacca fer repairs, an' I hadn't been ashore an hour when a squad o' marines nabbed me. I swum ashore in Fayal, two years after."

That was all Jeff could persuade him to tell. But there was a grim tightening of the seaman's jaws, when he spoke of that time, that gave the boy a hint of something deeper.

They had two days of good sailing with a northerly wind behind them. Mr. Jones had voiced some uneasiness about cruisers off Norfolk, but a dark night favored them, and they passed the mouth of the Chesapeake without trouble.

Jeff had heard plenty of tales from sailormen about storms off Cape Hatteras. On this voyage, however, Captain Preble prudently decided to use the inside passage. They cruised in shoal water off the sandy islands of Carolina all one morning, taking soundings every few minutes. At noon the lookout reported a break in the shoreline. Feeling their way in, they found the channel at last, and an hour later were sailing down the calm waters of Pamlico Sound.

The Yankee skipper was no slave-driver. Their luck in coming so far without molestation had put him in a mellow mood, and he decided to make a stop at Beaufort to get his crew fresh meat and provisions. When he returned to the schooner from his trip ashore he had a crate with a dozen fat chickens in the small-boat.

The mulatto cook outdid himself that night. He dressed four of the fowls and the men dined on savory fried chicken and boiled yams. At daylight next morning they weighed anchor and put out to sea.

Amos Gilman had been in the boat's crew that rowed the captain ashore. He gave Jeff a piece of news as they stood their trick at the wheel together in the freshening dawn breeze.

"We was fair lucky to leave port this mornin'," he remarked. "Feller in the tavern in B-B-Beaufort was sayin' Congress called a ninety-day embargo of all ships, startin' the first of April. That was a week ago, 'cordin' to my reckonin'. We cleared Gloucester just in time, an' if there'd been any g-g-gov'ment offi-cers in Beaufort yesterday we'd ha' been held."

He whistled cheerfully. "At that, we ain't doin' so bad," he told Jeff. "Halfway to Cuba now, an' we've run through the worst of it al-ready. Might sight a British cruiser down 'round the Bahamas, b-b-but they're makin' most o' their trouble to the north, outside the big ports."

"That's right," said Jeff. "Wait till we sell our codfish an' lumber in Havana, an' load up with hogsheads o' molasses. That cargo ought to bring twice over what the *Abigail's* worth, back in Portsmouth!"

That was a day of easy sailing for the wind was light and abeam. Jeff spent the watch below writing a letter to his father and a stiff little note to Patience Deering. He wished, now, that he had thought of letters earlier. He could have sent them ashore with the captain in Beaufort. But there might be a packet sailing from Havana while they lay in harbor, and mail would reach home ahead of him.

When he came back on deck for the first dog-watch he found the ship becalmed. The wind had died and the sea was smooth. Overhead and to the southward the sky was a smoky gray. The sun, which had been bright and hot in the forenoon, was wholly obscured now, so that they drifted in a queer half twilight on a lead-colored ocean.

The skipper stayed on the afterdeck talking to the mate. He wrinkled his nose and sniffed to port and starboard. "I tell ye, Ephraim," he said, "she don't smell right to me. Air's heavy. When ye git in this latitude that means hurricanes."

Mr. Jones squinted aloft and spat a golden stream over the side. "Don't take on so, Josiah," he replied mildly. " 'Tain't the hurricane season —not fer two-three months yet. Mebbe we'll git a squall or so, but I cal'late that's all."

Grumbling, the captain went below, only to reappear again in a few moments. "Glass is fallin'," he announced glumly. "I want all hands on deck. We'll try to make what we can to wind'ard 'fore the storm hits. Then we'll have to shorten sail in an almighty hurry."

A long, uneasy swell set in, and little puffs of wind, coming from nowhere, made cat's-paws on the gray surface of the water. The full crew sweated at the sails, hauling as the wind shifted. And the helm was put over half a dozen times in an hour as the schooner made sluggish headway to the eastward.

They ate hastily and in silence, two or three men going below at a time. Night came early and black as a hat. As the swell increased, the vessel's motion became a series of long hesitating climbs and dizzy downward swoops. And the wind grew. It whined in the shrouds and bellied the canvas in sudden gusts. At four bells in the first night watch Captain Preble ordered the topsails taken in and the main and foresails double-reefed.

It was a lucky move, for in less than an hour there came a lightning-like shift in the wind. Without warning, a full gale slammed out of the southwest. It caught the schooner close-hauled and almost threw her on her beam ends. Jeff dragged himself out of the scuppers and clung to a loose end of rope while the hurt ship slowly righted herself. The mainsail had been ripped from the top lashings, and now trailed over the side in a snarl of cordage, while the gaff swung crazily in the shrieking wind. Forward the single jib was gone—blown out and away by that burst of storm.

Wet to the skin and dazed by the suddenness of the catastrophe, Jeff groped his way to the fore shrouds and gripped them with shaky hands. Under the straining foresail the schooner wore to and was caught instantly in the trough of a sea. Tons of water came over the side with a solid crash, nearly tearing the boy loose from his hold. He braced himself against the drag of the receding sea and wiped the spray out of his eyes.

Aft, Nate Winslow and the mate were hacking at the tangle of wreckage. Captain Preble and two other men had the wheel hard down, endeavoring to bring her head to the wind. And someone—he thought it was Jonas Beale—was halfway up the mainmast, struggling with the fouled gaff halyards. Then he saw a corner of the big tarpaulin that covered the deck lumber tug loose from its lashings. With a vision of the whole mass of cargo blowing into the ocean, Jeff let go of the shrouds and darted across the lurching deck.

Scrambling to the top of the lumber pile he crawled aft till he could get his fingers on the edge of the whipping canvas. Twice the heavy cloth, stiff with tar and salt, jerked out of his grasp. The loose boards were lifting under him when he finally clutched the tarpaulin and started worming his way forward with it. His fingertips were raw and bleeding but he would not release his grip. The fore-boom slatted across, barely missing his head, and the schooner rolled her scuppers under to the savage thrust of another beam sea.

Jeff struggled to the forward end of the stack and dropped to the deck, still clinging to the drenched canvas. "Amos!" he yelled, with what breath he had left. "Get a rope—quick!"

Amos Gilman could never have heard his call above the shriek of the gale, but he saw what Jeff was doing. In a moment he was there, scrambling down the slant of the pitching deck. Somewhere he had snatched up a coil of stout line, and in a moment he was bending it to a corner of the tarpaulin. When it was firmly lashed in place, Jeff stumbled to his feet. His cramped fingers were bent like talons.

Amos steadied him against the rush of the next wave, and when it had passed they staggered forward to the shelter of the forecastle hatch. Gradually the terrific force of the wind was changing the direction of the seas. By turns, the schooner rolled in the trough and took the battering of the waves over her bow. At each shock she trembled as if she had struck a reef, and the toppling surges ran aft along her decks in a waist-deep flood.

CLEAR FOR ACTION!

Staring through the blown spray Jeff saw the lumber pile heave under its canvas cover. Lifted by the torrents of water beneath, the planks were beginning to float loose from their moorings. The boy groaned as he saw all his efforts going for nothing. Winslow and the mate were fighting their way forward now, and the down-easter had an ax in his hand. Without hesitation he brought the blade down on the very rope that Jeff and Amos had made fast. As the canvas whirled back, flying boards filled the air.

"Look," Amos shouted in Jeff's ear. "They're goin' to make a s-s-sea-anchor!"

Under the guidance of the mate, three or four of the crew dragged together two long planks and lashed them in the form of a cross. They braced the angles with smaller boards, then laboriously tied the corners of the tarpaulin to the four points of the cross. The work was constantly interrupted by breaking seas and gusts of wind. At last, however, they made the contrivance fast to a cable and succeeded in launching it over the side.

Captain Preble wrestled his way forward. Clinging to the foreshrouds, he shielded his eyes with one hand and watched the snaky, wet length of the cable. The schooner's bowsprit still swung in crazy arcs as she fell off the wind.

"Gol durn!" screamed the skipper. "It ain't holdin'! Haul in, you lubbers—we got to try again!"

At the end of twenty minutes of back-breaking work they got the sea-anchor alongside. It was too cumbersome to pull aboard, but they managed to attach a length of heavy chain to one corner and let the thing go again. The weight, intended to keep the drag from floating on top of the water, seemed to accomplish its purpose. After a few more swings into the trough, the *Abigail* steadied, bucking the seas head on.

It was now some time after midnight and the gale had not slackened in force. If anything, its violence increased as the hours passed. On the other hand there was little to be done on deck as long as the sea-anchor kept the schooner's head to wind.

Preble posted a lookout forward and stayed by the wheel with two seamen to help him. The rest of the crew he sent below to get what rest they could. Battered and soaked by their continual drenchings, it was a weary bunch of sailors who stumbled down the ladder into the welter of the forecastle. The storm lamp had been smashed and their narrow quarters were black as pitch. Feeling his way forward, Jeff barked his shins on a sea-chest that had slipped its moorings and was sliding to and fro between the berths. Clothing and blankets lay everywhere.

Wet as he was, the boy heaved himself into his disordered bunk. The pitching and shaking of the ship—the groan of straining timbers and the howl of the hurricane overhead—none of these could keep the tired lad awake. He flung an arm about the stanchion so that he would not be thrown out, and fell instantly into a stupor of sleep.

CHAPTER IV

Iᴛ ᴡᴀѕ three or four hours later when Jeff was rudely awakened by a blow on the head. Groping dazedly around him in the dark, he felt the edge of a bunk cutting into his back, then lost contact with it again as the schooner rolled. With a crash he landed against the stanchion of the opposite berth and clung there, trying to collect his wits.

Others of the crew, likewise shaken out of

their sleep, were grumbling curses as the pendulum-swing hurled them this way and that.

"All hands out!" a voice yelled down the open hatch. "We've lost the blasted sea-anchor!"

Stiff and aching in his still-wet clothes, Jeff hauled himself over to the ladder and climbed with the rest. The rain had stopped, but the screaming rush of the wind was wilder than ever and the *Abigail* rolled her scuppers under as each great wave went past. Clutching at anything that offered a handhold, the men fought to set a storm jib and slacked off on the foresail sheet. Without the drag there was nothing for it but to run before the gale or be swamped.

Now that her deck-load was gone, the schooner rode more buoyantly. Some water still came aboard, but it was mostly in the form of sheets of spray, whipped off the tops of those mountainous seas. When she was in the valley between two waves they loomed mast-high before and behind her.

It took two good men at the wheel to keep the vessel from broaching to, as she slithered down one foaming hillside after another. And four more hands were always at the pumps working desperately in half-hour shifts to hold down the rising water in her hold.

Jeff hardly noticed the passage of time. There was no daybreak—no real day. The black gloom changed only enough to show the furrowed peaks of waves and the dark, hurrying smother overhead. At the end of each trick at the pumps, the boy tumbled into a corner of the deck, too exhausted to move. Once in the course of that wild day the cook came on deck with a bucket of hot soup and ladled it out to each man. Somehow—nobody asked how—he had made a fire in the galley stove and brought water to a boil. The soup itself was an unsavory mess, but they gulped it gratefully, too tired and too hungry to be critical.

While Jeff was helping Amos Gilman at the wheel some time in the afternoon, he heard the captain arguing with Mr. Jones about their position.

"I tell ye the log ain't wuth a durn in this

sea!" the irate skipper was shouting. "I'd trust dumb guesswork quicker!"

"All right, Josiah—all right," the mate tried to soothe him. "If ye want my guess, we've drifted nigh onto thirty leagues a'ready. An' providin' the compass ain't bewitched, the wind's been sou'east from the start. I'll grant ye it's a fool direction fer a hurricane but this ain't no ordinary storm. Should ha' blowed herself out 'fore this, but look at her now!"

There was no sign of the gale's abating, then or the next morning. The crew stumbled about their tasks like sleepwalkers. To Jeff, when he had time to think about it at all, it seemed like a miracle that they kept the battered little craft afloat. If he looked astern into the stinging wind there was always a wave towering there, bigger and more menacing than any that had gone before. This time surely they must be swamped. Then with a heaving forward tilt the schooner would be climbing the dizzy slope, stern-first.

The worst moment always came when the crest passed under them and the deck fell away sickeningly from under their feet.

"How fast d'you reckon we're traveling?" the boy asked Nate Winslow that night.

The big sailor shook his head. "No way to tell," he said. "The whole ocean's movin', an' us with it. Might be ten knots—might be more. But anyhow, we're plenty off our course."

It was forty-eight hours before the force of the great wind slackened. The morning of the third day they were able to get sail on the schooner and turn her head southward once more, but the seas still ran too high for comfort. At noon the mate had a chance to shoot the sun and work out a position.

He came on deck after a half hour of heavy going with paper and pencil. "Mebbe I'm crazy," he told the captain, "but I make it thirty-three north an' sixty-nine-thirty west. That'd be nigh onto five hundred miles we was blowed. 'Tain't right nor reasonable, but there's the figgers."

"Gosh a'mighty!" yelped the skipper, clawing at his whiskers. "Only forty leagues from the

Bermudas! Git them tops'ls h'isted—quick! We ain't got a bit o' business in these waters."

The wind grew lighter and finally died out completely. There was plenty to be done aboard the schooner, however. Most of the crew were sent aloft to repair the havoc wrought by the storm. Stays and running rigging alike had suffered endless damage. Up on the fore-topmast, fifty feet above the deck, Jeff found himself swinging in dizzy arcs to the heave of the great swell. He spliced and tied and rove new lines through battered blocks. Below him, on the forecastle head, Amos Gilman and the ship's carpenter were hammering and sawing in an effort to patch up a hole that had been stove in the small-boat.

At eight bells in the afternoon a little breeze began to stir out of the northwest. It freshened and filled the ragged sails and the schooner bore away on a long slant to the southward.

Jeff had the first dogwatch below and came up yawning after he had eaten his supper. It was a help to eat decent food again, but he was still aching with weariness from lack of sleep and the beating he had taken during the storm. Now, in the warm sunset, he had difficulty in keeping his eyes open. But there was to be no rest, this watch.

"Up in the main crosstrees, youngster," called Mr. Jones. "Cap'n wants a sharp lookout to-night."

The lad grumbled a little to himself as he clambered upward. He wondered if he would ever get used to taking his sleep in three or four hour snatches. Back home in Maine he hadn't fully appreciated the luxury of a solid night's slumber. What wouldn't he give right now to roll into bed at dark and sleep right through till sunup!

A moment's thought made him ashamed. He had wanted the adventure of the sea and he was getting it. Any sailor worth his salt could learn to stand watches. He made himself as comfort-able as he could on his lofty perch and stared off to the east and south. Westward it was impos-sible to see anything, for the glare of the low sun made a dazzling brightness on the waves.

The breeze was fresh and pleasant now, and the schooner lay over to it so that her rolling was less noticeable. Jeff hung there for an hour and more, shifting position when his cramped legs went to sleep. And he kept a good watch. From rim to rim the sea was empty of anything but tossing waves. After a while there came a change in the light. He looked to the west and saw the red disc of the sun already cut in two by the horizon. In another moment it would be swallowed up in the ocean. He decided to count a hundred and see if it was gone.

The glow had faded when he looked again. But there on the edge of the violet sea—right where the sun had set—he saw something else. It was a tiny speck of sail, etched sharp against the sky.

Jeff freed his right arm and pointed. "Sail, ho!" he yelled. "Hull down to wind'ard."

"What is she?" asked the mate. "Can ye make her out?"

The boy shaded his eyes and peered intently

for a moment. "Square-rigged," he answered, "and she's got t'gallan's'ls and royals set. Comin' down fast by the look of her."

The captain had heard the hail and come on deck. Now he scuttled halfway up the ratlines with his spyglass under his arm. After a long look at the approaching sail he snapped out a string of orders. The wheel was spun, the fore and main sheets slacked off, and the schooner fell away before the wind.

They footed along southeastward at a good eight knots while the twilight deepened and the sea grew shadowy astern. If the other vessel gained on them at all it could not be noticed. When she finally disappeared in the gloom she was still too far away to be identified.

Captain Preble rubbed his hands and winked at the mate. "Let 'em figger we're runnin' off to loo'ard," said he. "Soon as it's good an' dark we'll come about on our course again."

Jeff was asleep in his berth before this strategy was put into effect. When he came on deck at midnight, however, the *Abigail* was close-hauled and her bowsprit pointed in the direction of Cuba. The breeze held true. If the other ship had been pursuing the schooner it seemed certain she had lost her quarry, for the night was dark.

The mate's watch was roused out at six with only two hours' sleep. "What in thunder's wrong now?" growled Amos. "It ain't a storm, that's sure. Look at the sunshine comin' in that open port!"

They scrambled abovedecks, rubbing sleepy eyes, and saw a knot of men gathered aft by the starboard rail. They were all looking and pointing to windward. There in the clear morning light stood a tall ship, her tapering masts crowded with white canvas, a creamy ribbon of foam sheering under her bows. She lay on a course parallel to the *Abigail's* and less than two miles on the weather beam.

"L-l-look at them guns!" breathed Amos. "A frigate, sure as shootin'!"

Jeff was staring at the broad white stripe along the ship's side and counting the black squares of the open gun-ports. Eleven of them—

and eight more in the pierced bulwarks above. A thirty-eight-gun frigate!

She was a beautiful sight, her cordage taut and fine, her yards trimmed to perfection and every sail drawing. There was a pennant flying from her main truck but it was whipped straight toward them by the breeze and showed only an occasional flash of color.

"What is she, British?" asked Jeff.

Nate Winslow was standing beside him. He nodded without speaking. His jaw was set in a hard ridge under the brown skin. Before the big seaman turned away Jeff saw the look of desperation in his eyes.

Aft, the knot of watchers broke up suddenly. Captain Preble's agitated voice shrilled on the morning air. "Ease the main sheet an' git ready to jibe the fores'l!" he cried. "Jump to it, ye lubbers, 'less ye want to be boarded!"

They worked like madmen then, all thought of bed and breakfast forgotten. With the schooner running before the wind, her main and foresails spread like a pair of wings, they seemed to be holding their distance. There was no longer any doubt that the frigate was in pursuit of them. She had immediately changed course and was driving along like a tall white cloud in their wake.

"Stuns'ls! She's settin' stuns'ls!" came Amos Gilman's shout from the crosstrees. Looking astern, Jeff could see a broadening of the pillar of canvas on the ship-of-war. With the added drive of the studding-sails she began to gain, little by little.

"Ain't but one thing to do now, Josiah," the mate remarked coolly. "We're carryin' all the sail we got. How 'bout lightenin' ship—tossin' over some o' the cargo?"

"No, no!" the skipper wailed. "We can't do that, Eph! The profits o' the hull v'yage? Let the spare anchor go—an' the chain cable. But don't tech that codfish—not yet. Mebbe we'll fetch Havana when we've shaken 'em off."

The heavy storm anchor went overboard with a mighty splash, and half the chain in the locker followed it. The squat little *Abigail* lifted her bows like a rearing horse and charged ahead with added speed. The shift in her ballast had brought her down by the stern, but as long as she ran before the wind that was no handicap.

Every man on deck except the helmsman was watching the race with breathless absorption. "We're gainin'!" Jonas Beale cried. "Hooray fer the old *Abigail!*"

Mr. Jones shook his head. "Ain't time to crow yet," he said. "We're holdin' our own but mighty little more." He paused and gave emphasis to his words by shooting a jet of tobacco juice over the rail. "Remember—they don't have to git but about a cable's length closer 'fore they kin start target-practice with that bow-chaser."

All through the morning the pursuit continued. Sometimes the schooner seemed to pull away a little. Then again a flaw in the wind would let the man-o'-war creep nearer. Toward noon the breeze began to fail. The log showed their speed dropping from ten knots to nine— then seven—then a sluggish three or four. Captain Preble hopped back and forth on his little

THE "ABIGAIL" CHARGED AHEAD WITH ADDED
SPEED

quarterdeck and fumed at the weather.

"Gol-ding it!" he yelped. "Why don't it come on to blow or else give us a flat calm? We could beat the blasted Britisher in a towin' match!"

But the wind did not die entirely. It came in light, uncertain puffs—"flighty as a gal at her first huskin'-bee," as the mate put it. And little by little the frigate closed the gap between them. Her lofty royals caught more air than the schooner could hope to find. Jeff stared fascinated at the gleaming black hull of the cruiser and the crisp white of the bow-wave, trampled under her forefoot. As he watched, a round, cottony cloud unfolded at the ship's prow. Slow seconds passed and then the hollow *boom* of a cannon sounded across the blue water. Something came skipping over the waves to disappear in a fountain of spray twenty yards off the schooner's starboard quarter.

"She's in range," the captain said, more quietly than Jeff had ever heard him speak. " 'Tain't no use, Eph. Haul yer sheets an' put the helm up. We're goin' to heave to."

CHAPTER V

THE *Abigail* came lurching around with her head to the wind. The frigate was now only half a mile away and coming down fast considering the light air. They saw her topmen scampering aloft like little dark ants, and in a moment the royals and topgallant-sails were clued up to the yards. As she drew within a cable's length she swung broadside on in a graceful sweep. Hardly had she hove to before her longboat dropped to the water and a dozen rowers gave way smartly.

"That's an officer o' marines in the stern-sheets," Amos muttered in Jeff's ear. "See that there red c-c-coat a-shinin'?"

"What'll they do when they get here?" Jeff asked. "You don't reckon they'd have sunk us, do you—if we hadn't stopped?"

Amos shrugged. "Ain't no tellin'," he said. "We'll s-s-see what they're up to, soon enough."

Indeed, the longboat was alongside in two more strokes. The crew of the *Abigail* stood in stony silence while the Englishmen clambered to the deck. The red-faced young lieutenant of marines came first, followed by a boatswain and four stalwart seamen.

The officer wrinkled his nose at the smell of salt cod wafted from the hold. "Come, come," he snapped pettishly. "Who's in command here?"

Josiah Preble stepped forward with a certain dignity. "I am," he answered. "Cap'n Preble, schooner *Abigail,* Shinnequid, Maine."

"And a cargo of fish, eh? Making for some port in the West Indies, I'll be bound!"

The skipper held his peace. "Come, answer up, man!" barked the Englishman.

"No," lied Preble, stoutly. "We cleared fer Savannah. Got blowed off our course in that gale."

"Ha!" The officer laughed without mirth. "Everyone knows you Yankees try to trade with the islands because you know your smelly codfish is wanted for the slaves. Well, we'll see that you're headed for Savannah right enough. Now line up your crew here. We're looking for British seamen."

The Americans made no movement until they saw the mate nod. Then they straggled forward to stand in an uneven row. Jeff stepped up with the rest. He felt a little shiver run down his spine. This was it—the thing they had been dodging all down the coast.

The big, hard-faced, British bo'sun was grinning maliciously now. He strode forward a pace. "You," he said, pointing a stubby finger at

Jonas Beale. "Born in good ol' England, I'll warrant. Step out 'ere an' let's 'ave a look at yer."

Beale's black brows came together in a scowl. "No, sir," he muttered. "I ain't no bloody Britisher—"

The bo'sun made a quick movement and struck him hard across the mouth. "No insults in front o' one of 'is Majesty's orficers!" he growled. "Ye're a Bristol man. I've seen yer before. What abaht it, men?"

"Aye," chorused the four seamen. "Bristol 'e are. Tell it by 'is talk."

They seemed to relish the proceedings as much as their superiors. Jeff saw one of them wink at his companions.

"Why, gol durn it!" Beale blurted, "it's much as I kin do to understand yer blasted lingo!" He wiped the blood off his cut lip and subsided, as the bo'sun made another threatening gesture.

"Put him in the boat, men," ordered the lieutenant. "He's English, and he'll have a chance to serve his king as all honest Englishmen should."

The big Yankee was seized by the arms and hustled over the side before he could make further protest.

Jeff wet his lips and looked along the line. Suddenly he realized that Nate Winslow was not in sight. He nudged Amos Gilman. "Where's Nate?" he whispered out of the side of his mouth.

The other boy turned his head, glancing behind him, and the marine officer saw the movement.

"What's this?" he barked. "Someone missing? Durkin, take a man with you and search the ship. Have a look into all their cursed hiding-places!"

While the bo'sun was carrying out the order below, the lieutenant strutted up and down the deck, eying the line of sullen Americans disdainfully. "Pretty poor stuff," he remarked, "but some of you have known the feel of a navy cat, I'll warrant."

He sized up Gilman's awkward bulk and

Jeff's solid shoulders. "You two," he indicated them with a jerk of his thumb. "How long since you left England?"

"M-m-me?" stammered Amos. "I wan't never there, l-l-let alone leavin' there!"

"Come, come," the officer snapped. "What's that tattooed on your arm? An anchor, eh? Don't tell me you got that in the Province of Maine. Look at it, Jenks. Suggest anything to you?"

A heavy-set tar with a face that was scarred by powder-burns stepped forward at the word. He squinted at the tattooed anchor with the eye of a connoisseur. "Ye're right, sir," he said. "I'd know that 'ere work any place. Done in Madam Spilligo's at Plymouth, that was. An' don't try to deny it, young bucko! Wot say, Leftenant? In the boat?"

The marine officer nodded and two stalwart sailors swung the struggling lad over the rail. A feeling of desperation came over Jeff as the lieutenant's eye fell coldly on him.

"You, there," came the order. "What's your name?"

"Jeffrey Robbins, Shinnequid."

"Born there, I suppose?" There was obvious irony in the question.

"Yes."

One of the seamen interrupted roughly. "Say 'sir,' an' none o' yer impidence," he growled.

White with anger, Jeff gritted his teeth and said nothing.

"It's easy to see he's lying," the officer remarked with a bored smile. "He didn't get his build from eating Yankee fish and beans. That's good British beef."

Jeff had already seen the futility of argument. There was no place to run to, and if he put up a fight the odds against him would be overwhelming. He looked around at the other Americans, but in their faces he saw only blank despair.

At that moment Durkin and his companion returned to the afterdeck. "No sign of any men below, sir," the bo'sun reported. "We 'unted through the lockers an' the cargo 'old, too, sir."

"Hm." The lieutenant fingered his shaven

chin. "That's odd. I'd have sworn there was something going on here." He looked aloft, then at the rail. "I have it!" he exclaimed. "Overboard —search the rudder chains and the bow tackle!"

Two of the seamen ran forward and two aft. " 'Ere 'e is!" came a shout from the taffrail. "In the water, 'angin' to the rudder."

It took only a moment or two for them to drag Nate Winslow up over the schooner's quarter. He stood there dripping, the hair hanging lank on his forehead. There was a wild look in his eyes, and his lips were drawn back from his teeth like those of a cornered wolf.

The lieutenant of marines stared at him strangely. "I'd swear I'd seen this man somewhere," he said, and Jeff knew that for once he meant it.

"Have you ever served in an English ship?" the officer asked.

To Jeff's surprise, his friend made no denial. "Yes, sir," he answered huskily. "I made one voyage in the brig *Nancy,* out o' Halifax."

"Merchantman, eh?" The lieutenant wrinkled his brows. "You never sailed aboard a man-o'-war?"

Winslow's face was blank. "No, sir," he said.

For several seconds the marine continued to study him as if trying to remember something. Then he swung brusquely on his heel. "Take him and the boy there," he commanded. "We've got the best of them. The rest are old men and scrubs."

"Please, sir—" Jeff stepped forward, "—could we take our dunnage along?"

"Yes," the officer nodded carelessly. "Go with 'em, Durkin, and have 'em bring what belongs to the other two men."

The bo'sun, backed up by Jenks and another man-o'-warsman, followed Jeff and Nate down the forecastle companion. It took the boy only a minute to stuff his belongings into his sea-bag. His hand shook as he touched the wool vest knitted by Patience Deering—the gift he had never had a chance to wear. He gathered Amos Gilman's things together while Winslow was collecting his own and Jonas Beale's. Staggering under their load of bags and sea-chests, they reached the deck and walked through the silent group of Yankee seamen.

Jeff turned to Preble as he climbed over the rail. "Let my dad know, will you, Cap'n?" he said. And he had time to see the old man nod before the bo'sun shoved him roughly on his way.

The prisoners—for in everything but name they were prisoners—crouched where they could find room on the rowing thwarts. The oarsmen seemed to find their predicament amusing. At least there was some good-natured joshing as they shot across the waves to the frigate. Jeff turned his head and saw her high, black, gleaming side lifting above him—her open ports and the ugly snouts of the long eighteen-pounders thrusting from her gun-deck. They swung under her quarter and he saw above him the stern gallery and the raised gilt letters of the name— "H.M.S. ALBATROSS." Under his breath, the boy said it over to himself. A fine, free-sounding name for a ship. It had a kind of fearless *swoop* to it. He wondered if he would come to hate that name.

. . . .

It was about two in the afternoon when the four Yankees climbed the swaying Jacob's ladder to the frigate's deck. Leaving their dunnage in the alley between two carronades, they were marched aft to stand before the first officer, a stout and jolly-faced young man, addressed as Lieutenant Cottington.

He was in a good humor about something and it took him a little time to put himself in a suitably serious frame of mind. He pursed his lips, puckered his brows and looked up from the little table where he had been at work.

"Hrrrmph!" he grunted. "I understand you men have volunteered for enlistment in His Majesty's Navy. Very creditable, I'm sure— hrrmph! Your names, please. I'll read you the Articles of War and have you entered on the ship's roll."

The formalities were quickly over and the new seamen of the *Albatross* were turned over to the tender mercies of Boatswain Durkin. He herded them forward and pointed to a corner of the 'tween-decks. "Ye'll sling yer 'ammocks 'ere," he announced. "Be on deck in three minutes. I'll instruct ye in some o' yer duties aboard a man-o'-war."

Beale was still sulking and Winslow maintained his white-faced silence, but Jeff was already shaking off the daze of the calamity that had befallen them. Perhaps because he knew so little about life in the royal navy, he could forget his predicament and look about him with interest.

The whole space in the 'tween-decks seemed to be crowded with cannon. The slides and tackle of the long guns left only a narrow alleyway amidships running from mainmast to foremast. But between the guns were countless neatly stowed hammocks. Apparently the whole crew was quartered here.

When the four Yankees climbed blinking to the open deck the frigate was running close-hauled on a westerly course. Under her lee the little *Abigail* crawled along on the light breeze, her patched, gray canvas flapping dispiritedly. Staring after the schooner, Jeff was suddenly brought back to his present surroundings by a stinging pain in his thigh.

"That'll wake ye up," snapped the bo'sun's hard voice. "An' ye'll feel plenty more of it before I've done with ye." In his hand Jeff saw a short length of rope with a heavy knot in the end. "This 'ere is wot we calls a 'starter,'" the bo'sun nodded, shaking the rope meaningly. "It's a big 'elp to slow-witted lubbers like you."

He put his big fists on his hips and glowered at the quartet. "Now," he barked, "stand to attention! You"—he jerked his head toward Beale—"are in the larboard watch. The rest of ye are starboard. For now, though, ye'll all come with me to learn yer stations. Answer up, there!"

"Aye, aye, sir," Nate Winslow responded, and the others followed his lead in timid chorus.

There were more than two hundred men busy about the deck but none of them paid any attention to their new shipmates as the bo'sun led his little squad forward. Tersely he pointed out their battle stations and topmen's duties. Both the youngsters were assigned to the foretop, Nate and Jonas, as more experienced sailors, going to the main.

The bo'sun had his own methods of testing seamanship. "Let's see ye go aloft," he ordered Jeff and Amos. "Lively, now!"

They jumped for the weather foremast shrouds and scurried upward like a couple of frightened squirrels. Jeff reached the crosstrees first and stopped to look down.

"Keep on!" roared Durkin. "I said 'aloft,' didn't I?"

Leaving Amos to make his own lumbering progress, Jeff caught the topgallant shrouds and sped on. He was panting and dizzy when he got to the fore royal truck. He clung to the ratlines and felt the sway of the tall mast. The sea swirled clear and green, a hundred and thirty feet below him.

"Now then—down, in a hurry—out o' that other lummox's way!" came the bo'sun's distant shout.

Jeff knew there was no room for both of them on the narrowed shrouds at the top. He reached for the taut backstay, wrapped his legs around it, and slid. The swift descent took his breath away, burned his hands and left his breeches smoking, but he got a thrill out of it. He found himself back on the deck in a quarter of the time it had taken him to go aloft.

Durkin was still occupied in watching Amos' clumsy efforts and roaring curses at the unfortunate lad, so that Jeff had time to cool his palms and catch his breath. It was only a moment's respite, however.

"Look 'ere," the bo'sun began as soon as Amos reached the deck, "supposin' the order was to back the fore top's'l—what'ud ye do? Show me, now!"

Jeff ran to the weather braces and laid his hand on a rope.

"Not that 'un, ye fool!" yelled Durkin, swinging his starter threateningly. "That's the fore-course halyard!"

A glance aloft showed the boy his mistake and he corrected it quickly. So the lesson went on. Jeff learned fast and Amos, who had sailed in a square-rigger before, was already familiar with most of the ropes and their uses.

At the end of an hour a call was passed forward from the quarterdeck and Durkin put his pipe to his lips. Two bo'sun's mates took up the shrill whistling and the crew came on the run from every part of the ship.

"All hands to exercise at the guns," barked Durkin. " 'Ere, you two blarsted farmers—get to stations!" He swung the rope's end smartly about Amos' legs and the boys rushed to take their places. They had been assigned to different gun-crews but both of them were in the port battery of carronades, on the open boat-deck. Jeff's gun-captain was a grim-faced Scot named MacGregor. There was nothing dashing about his stoop-shouldered figure but—as the boy soon learned—he had the reputation of being the best gun-layer in the ship.

They had a minute or two before the order

was passed to clear for action, and into those fleeting seconds MacGregor poured all his eloquence in an effort to explain Jeff's duties. The boy's ears were buzzing when the drum rolled out the signal. He sprang to the breeching as he had been told, and helped haul back the short, heavy thirty-two-pounder. Two of his mates had already dropped the bulwark section in front of the gun's mouth. To the rhythmic intonation of the Scotsman's commands, they rammed home a make-believe wad and cartridge, went through the motions of shotting the cannon, ran it out with a desperate heave on the tackle, and pointed the blunt muzzle at an imaginary target. MacGregor was as particular about his aim as if he were trying to sink an enemy ship of the line. "Na use o' wastin' powder, even if 'tis but an exercise," he was given to telling his crew.

Gunnery Lieutenant Brown, in charge of the port side battery, looked along the line, lifted his hand and brought it down with a sharp command. "Fire!"

The lanyards were pulled in unison, and so

real was the action that Jeff half braced himself for the deafening roar of the broadside.

"Next time, 'ang on to that breechin'!" the man next to him panted in his ear as they hove the carronade back. "The recoil's somethin' terrible on these thirty-twos."

They swabbed out the gun, went through the motions of reloading, and were ready again when the command came. Five imaginary broadsides were fired in succession. Then, at the twitter of the bo'suns' pipes, the sweating crews stood at attention. From the quarterdeck a figure in a blue, epauletted coat, snowy breeches and cocked hat, addressed them in a clear, disdainful voice.

"Twelve minutes, fifty seconds. Much too slow. Mr. Brown, I shall expect better time hereafter."

The lieutenant saluted and turned glowering to give the gun-captains a dressing-down.

"Was that your skipper?" Jeff asked the sailor beside him.

The man laughed at the word. "Better not let

'im 'ear yer call 'im that!" he advised. "Aye, that's Cap'n St. John Frothingham, 'isself. 'E don't often speak to the likes of us, but w'en 'e does, step sharp!"

To a chorus of crackling orders the bulwarks were replaced and the slides of the carronades securely lashed to ring-bolts in the deck.

MacGregor came over to Jeff's side. "Ye're a quick hand," he said grudgingly. "Some day I might show ye a few o' the tricks o' gun-pointing."

At that moment there was a cry from overhead. "Deck, there!" the lookout called. "A squall's blowing up astern!"

"All hands to shorten sail," came Lieutenant Cottington's crisp order. And with a bare glimpse over his shoulder at the blackening sky, Jeff raced for the foremast rigging.

CHAPTER VI

THE TRAINED crew went aloft like lightning, jumping to the rapid-fire of orders that came from the deck below. "Take in courses and to'gallan's'ls!" yelled the mates. "Reef tops'ls! Stand by braces!"

Hurry as he would, Jeff found himself among the last to reach the fore-course yard. A monkey-faced twelve-year-old midshipman was there before him. "Out here!" he cried shrilly, and led the way along the foot-rope to the leeward end of the yard.

Jeff had never tried furling a square sail, and the huge fore-course was a tough beginning. He watched the little midshipman clawing valiantly at the canvas and put his own big hands to work in like fashion. The sheets had been slacked and after two or three futile grabs they succeeded in catching a handful of sail. Fortunately the squall had not yet overtaken the ship and they had little wind to contend with. A few clumsy attempts taught the Yankee boy to pull up as much canvas as he could hold at a time and snug it down between his belly and the swaying spar.

"Faster!" screamed the youngster at his side. "Look—the wind's coming!"

They labored frantically for a few more seconds and dragged in the jerking foot of the sail just as the full fury of the squall reached them. The midshipman whipped a gasket line around the bunchy canvas and passed the free end to Jeff who did the same, handing the gasket to the next man inboard. Then he had to cling for his

FOR AN INSTANT HE SWUNG WILDLY

life to the yard.

The wind had struck like a swooping hawk, bowing the groaning ship so far to leeward that the end of the spar pointed right down into an angry sea. For an instant the little fellow on the end of the yard was thrown clear of the foot-rope and swung wildly, holding to the gasket with one hand. Jeff shifted his own grip and reached down till he could seize the boy's wrist.

It seemed an eternity before the frigate righted herself, and when she did the pull of the midshipman's weight almost tore Jeff's arm out of its socket. Then they were high aloft once more and the frightened lad recovered his hold.

Shaky in the knees, Jeff made his way back along the yard and down the rigging. The crew had worked swiftly and well. With everything snugged down on deck, the frigate was racing along before the gale under reefed fore and main topsails.

Off to leeward and a mile ahead the boy could just make out the little Yankee schooner. Short-handed, she was making heavy weather of it. He saw that one of her topsails had blown out and was streaming away in tattered ribbons from the peak. It had been close to sunset when the squall struck. Now, under a black canopy of storm-clouds, night already seemed to be falling. Whipped by the wind, the waves were growing bigger, and the air was so full of driven spray that in a moment Jeff could no longer see the *Abigail*. He wondered then if he would ever see her again.

. . . .

The storm was still raging when the port watch went below for supper. Jeff stood in line to get his rations and stood in line to eat them, for no trestles had been put out on account of the pitching of the ship. Hungry as he was, he had little stomach for the fat salt pork, wormy ship's biscuit and pale, luke-warm tea that had been served out.

The Scotch gun-captain was beside him, eating with apparent relish. He saw Jeff eying the biscuit distastefully and offered some advice. "If ye dinna like the taste o' the weevils," he said, "juist gie the biscuit a smart tap or two. Then ye lay it doon for a meenit till they hae time to crawl oot."

When he had finished, MacGregor cut some tobacco from a black twist and rubbed it carefully between his palms preparatory to filling his pipe. "The food aboard a man-o'-war," he said, "is nae sae bad, on the whole. When we're six months oot o' port the bread and water get lively, but pork is always filling. And the lime-juice they gie us once a week keeps the scurvy doon."

He went to the galley stove for a light and came back puffing clouds of strong, pungent smoke. "The worst o' these long cruises," he continued, "is the shortage o' powder and shot. Gun practice wi'oot firin' canna train the eye. But the Admiralty rules gie us only one full round a month at the targets, and the Frenchies are so scarce, this side o' the water, that there's few chances to fire in action."

When the watch was called on deck again, Jeff found Nate Winslow just ahead of him on the ladder. The big American seaman motioned to him to follow and they went quietly over to the bulwark by the foremast shrouds. The squall had blown itself out but the sea was still running high and the night sky was murky. No sign of the *Abigail* could be seen on the dark horizon.

"I wanted a word with ye, lad," Nate whispered, when he was sure there was no one close enough to hear. "Ye'd better fergit anything I told ye back aboard the schooner. Ever hear what they do to deserters from the Royal Navy? A thousand lashes! A real stout man might live through a hundred. That's why I told 'em I'd been in a merchantman when they caught me. But that officer o' marines—that Porter—"

Jeff felt the big fellow shiver. "What about him?" he asked under his breath.

"He's tryin' to remember me," Nate answered. "We was both aboard the old *Invincible* once." He nudged Jeff and spat over the side as one of the bo'sun's mates strolled near.

" 'Ere, you two Yanks," growled the newcomer. "None o' yer schemin', now. Find a bit o' work to do or I'll find it for yer with a rope's end."

Nate yawned convincingly. "The wind's gone down," he said. "Ain't we goin' to make sail?"

"Gor!" sneered the bo'sun's mate. "I'll 'ave to pass the word to the cap'n. 'E'll be pleased, I'm sure, to know 'e's got a new sailin' marster aboard!"

Some of the edge was taken off his sarcasm by the order, relayed from the quarterdeck at that moment, to shake out reefs and set courses. The two New Englanders ran to their stations as the pipes shrilled, and a few seconds later Jeff was up on the yard once more. He found the young midshipman there beside him. As the last of the lashings was released and the big sail bellied out in the buntlines, the boy spoke in a squeaky, adolescent voice that he tried vainly to make impressive.

"That was good seamanship this afternoon, Robbins," he said. "Might have fallen off the yard but for you. I say—they're not over-fond of Yankees in this ship, but—I'll do what I can for you."

Jeff grinned in the dark. "Aye, aye, sir," he replied. "May I ask your name, sir?"

"Mr. Hammersley," the youngster answered with dignity. "We're all Navy—my people, I mean. I've been in the *Albatross* a year come Michaelmas, so perhaps I can help you get your bearings."

It was a strange system, Jeff thought, that sent little boys off to fight at sea, but he had to admire the pluck of young Mr. Midshipman Hammersley.

When he went below with Amos, at the change of the watch, they found three hundred hammocks slung in the cramped space of the 'tween-decks. The rings were eighteen inches apart. When a broad-shouldered seaman lay in his hammock he could hardly turn over without waking the sleeper on either side of him.

Nevertheless Jeff found his swinging canvas bed surprisingly comfortable. The frigate was pitching and rolling a good deal in the seas that had been raised by the squall, but the motion was far less noticeable than it would have been in a wooden berth.

Morning found the *Albatross* cruising south-westward before a fair sailing breeze. Jeff was put to work before daylight holystoning a section of deck in the waist of the ship. It was hard labor and the bo'sun's mate stood over the men with a rope's end, keeping them at it every minute. For that reason it was not until after sunrise that the boy had a chance to steal a glance at the sea. He was looking for the *Abigail*. But the sharp blue line of the horizon was clear of any sail. Either the little schooner had succeeded in giving them the slip or she had foundered in the gale.

The bell had just been struck for the end of the morning watch when a high-pitched twitter of pipes brought the men to attention.

Durkin, the bo'sun, was shouting an order. "All hands to witness punishment!"

They gathered from below and aloft, lining up six deep on either side of the 'midships gangway. Jeff felt a sudden sinking of the heart when he saw Jonas Beale stumbling aft between two husky bo'sun's mates.

"What is it—what did he do?" he whispered to Nate Winslow, close beside him.

Winslow was standing rigid, his face gray under the tan. Without turning, he breathed an answer through his teeth. "They're makin' an example of him—for the rest of us Yankees. That dirty Jenks put him to clearin' latrines. Tried to shove him in, an' Jonas lifted a fist to him."

The black-haired American was stripped to the waist, his burly back and shoulders white in the morning sun. They bent ropes to his wrists and hoisted him into the main rigging so that he stood on tiptoe.

Durkin read the sentence in a booming voice. "For refusal to obey an order—two dozen lashes."

A low, ominous sound began—the roll of a drum. As it reached a climax the cat-o'-nine-tails hissed through the air and the weighted thongs bit into Beale's back so that he jerked convulsively and cried out.

Silence, then deliberately the drum began to growl again. Jeff shuddered and tried to look away, but the bo'sun's cane jabbed him in the ribs.

"Eyes front, ye scum, an' watch the punishment!" was the low-voiced command.

Slowly the flogging dragged on. At the count of fifteen, the Yankee sailor hung limply from the wrist ropes. He no longer made any sound, but his body winced spasmodically and swayed to every blow. His back was a red smear.

Jeff felt sick and dizzy. His shaky knees barely held him up, and he wanted to scream aloud that they must stop the bloody business.

Nate Winslow's shoulder pressed against his own. "Steady, lad," he whispered. And by an effort of will the boy pulled himself together.

It was over at last. They let go the ropes, and Jonas Beale slumped down to the deck, unconscious. A kind of sigh went through the ranks of the assembled seamen. Some of them laughed self-consciously and others stretched their arms and swore.

Durkin lifted his pipe to his lips and blew a shrill blast. "All hands to breakfast!" he barked briskly.

Jeff never felt less appetite for a meal than for that breakfast. He nibbled at a biscuit and gulped a swallow or two of tea, but could not bring himself to touch the fat pork. He knew now how close he had come to fainting up there on deck, and shame was mixed with his anger.

The stoop-shouldered Scotch gunner came past and saw Jeff's pale, unhappy face. "Best eat a bit o' the sow-belly, lad," he urged kindly. "Ye'll be main hungry afore ye get anither meal."

Back on deck the clear, cool air of the sea soon straightened the boy out. Along with Amos and a couple of other members of the watch, he was set to polishing brass-work under the supervision of Midshipman Hammersley. It was a pleasant enough task. From the moment he came aboard, Jeff had admired the spotless cleanliness and order that prevailed aboard the man-o'-war. He saw now what made it possible. In fair weather three hundred men were kept occupied a large part of every day, scrubbing, painting and polishing, tarring and coiling down ropes. It was a prodigal use of labor that no merchantman could afford.

Six bells in the forenoon watch had been struck when the lookout in the fore-topmast shrouds hailed the deck.

"Sail, ho! Tops'l schooner, hull down on the starboard beam!"

The ship roused to instant activity as hands were called to man the braces. Up the rigging scampered a swarm of topmen to set the royals. To a succession of snapping commands the wheel was put over and the *Albatross* wore to on a course that would bring her across the stranger's bows.

For an hour the two vessels gradually drew closer together. There was no sign of sheering off on the part of the schooner. Nate Winslow watched her with interest. "Don't act very scairt, do they?" he remarked. "Might think they hadn't even sighted us."

"Maybe they're British," Jeff suggested, with a glance aloft at the frigate's bright ensign. "They must have spotted our flag before this."

But Winslow shook his head. "Look at the lines of her," he said. "An' the rake of her masts. That craft never come out of a British yard. Looks to me like one o' them fast Baltimore schooners. There—watch! She's spreadin' more sail!"

As if she had merely been playing with the *Albatross* up till then, the schooner flung out a cloud of white canvas forward—a balloon jib. A scant three miles away now, and nearly abeam, they could see the water leap under her sharp forefoot.

The warship held grimly to the chase but it was soon evident that she would be far astern when her course crossed that of the smaller vessel. It was midafternoon before Captain Frothingham decided to give up his pursuit. By that time the schooner was hull down in the west, her white sails no more than a tiny speck on the rim of the sea.

The men were piped to haul the yards around, and the frigate swung off to the southward with the wind on her port quarter.

That night in the peace of a fair-weather watch, young Hammersley greeted Jeff at his post by the fore shrouds. "A fine night, Robbins," said the midshipman, in his best quarter-deck manner. "We get them like this, sometimes, in the Gulf Stream." He leaned against the bulwark and in a moment he was a twelve-year-old once more.

"I say," he asked eagerly, "have you ever been to the West Indies?"

"Not me," said Jeff. "I've never been any place much, till this voyage. Just stayed all my life alongshore in Maine."

"I've never been there either," said the younger boy. "Not to go ashore, I mean. We sighted land in the Bahamas once, about a month ago. But we're heading down that way again. Leftenant Cottington showed us on the chart. We might put in at Nassau, this cruise—or even go as far as Jamaica. Did you ever chew a piece of sugar cane, Robbins?"

Jeff smiled in the darkness. "Yep," he replied. " 'Twasn't real fresh, but it sure was sweet. Uncle o' mine brought home a couple o' stalks of it from a coasting voyage when I was a little tad."

He looked at the pale oval of the impish young face and wondered.

"Maybe you can tell me something, Mr. Hammersley," he said. "Do they have punishment pretty often—like what we saw this morning?"

The midshipman nodded. "Yes," he said. "Helps preserve discipline and all that."

"Gee!" murmured Jeff. "I couldn't stand to watch it often—even if I didn't know the man being flogged!"

Young Hammersley stiffened. "You've got to be hard in the navy," he answered with grown-up gruffness. Then he laid an impulsive hand on Jeff's arm. "I know," he whispered. "It used to make me sick, too. What I do now is keep my eyes on the rigging just above their heads, and —and say the multiplication table!"

CHAPTER VII

THE DEEP, warm blue of the Gulf Stream was all around them during the next few days. The weather continued fine, and the breeze, never boisterous, was strong enough to keep them moving along at a good clip.

Little by little, Jeff began to adjust himself to the strange life aboard the frigate. At first, in his ignorance, he had broken some rule or other every few minutes, and his sides were sore from blows of the starter and the bo'sun's cane. But his wits were quick enough, and with a few hints from Winslow, MacGregor and his friend, the little midshipman, he was soon able to bear a hand about the ship without getting into difficulties.

For Amos Gilman it was a slower process. Strong as an ox, the poor lad was naturally clumsy in his movements, and his broad buttocks made a perfect target for a rope's end. Only his unfailing good nature kept him out of serious trouble. Nobody could hate Amos for long.

Aside from the daily scrubbing of decks, gun-practice and an occasional call to trim the yards, the crew had little to do. On Sunday morning Captain Frothingham inspected the ship and conducted a regular Church of England service from the quarterdeck. To Jeff's Yankee ear the hymns had a strange sound, but all hands sang lustily and he joined in whenever he knew the words.

In the afternoon a few of the men were allowed to bait hooks and trail them over the side.

The blue water was full of fish. There were little, brilliant-hued flying-fish that skipped and sailed under the frigate's bows. And once in a while Jeff could catch a glimpse of a bigger shape darting close to the surface in savage pursuit. For an hour there was little activity among the indolent fishermen along the bulwarks. Then suddenly they began yelling with excitement. As fast as they could haul the taut lines they pulled the fish aboard. The *Albatross* had sailed straight into a big school of bonito.

That night the 'tween-decks supped in style. Not even the ham-handed efforts of a man-o'-war cook could wholly spoil the flavor of that sweet, firm meat.

"If only there was some way o' saving the fish they catch," Jeff told Amos on deck, later, "we could have a change from salt horse once in a while. I don't mind this life much, except for the grub."

Amos sighed. "Sure," he answered, "I reckon you git on all right. You're q-q-quicker'n I be at things. But it ain't so bad in fair weather. You figger they'll k-k-keep us in the service all our lives?"

"They'll try," said Jeff. "What's to stop 'em? Did we have a chance to say whether we wanted to enlist? You bet we didn't. But"—he dropped his voice—"I don't aim to stay any longer'n I can help, do you?"

Amos shook his head doubtfully. "N-n-no," he replied. "Only how in time ye goin' to git off —in the middle o' the ocean?"

"She can't stay at sea all the time, can she? We'll just have to wait for a chance, that's all."

.   .   .   .

The easy routine of the cruise ended with unexpected suddenness next morning. Hardly had the sun come out of the sea when the lookout in the foretop hailed the deck. "Sail, ho!" he cried. "Dead to leeward!"

One of the junior lieutenants got an order from the quarterdeck and raced forward with a telescope. In a moment he was up in the fore-rigging, looking toward the southern horizon. On deck all heads were turned in the same direction. Jeff could just make out a spot of white there where the sky met the sea.

Lieutenant Cottington came forward to the foremast foot. "What d'you make her, Carlin?" he shouted.

"Merchant ship, sir, as near as I can tell. She's under full sail on the port tack. No—wait—she's falling off now! Going to run for it. Must have sighted us, sir, I should think."

"No colors?"

"No, sir, no colors—but from the cut of her sails she looks like a Frenchman!"

Hardly had the word passed his lips when the order for more sail came from the quarterdeck. To a squeaking of pipes they scurried aloft and set the royals, then the fore and main studding-sails. The breeze was fresh and steady. Five minutes after the other ship had been sighted, the *Albatross* was tearing along at a fine ten knots, her cordage creaking and her bow-wash curling back in white-flecked green ridges.

Meanwhile there was a thrill of excitement aboard the frigate. Jeff tingled all over as he awaited the call to clear for action. Now he was going to see some real fighting! They wouldn't be using make-believe powder and shot when they got the French ship under their guns. For by now the crew were positive it was an enemy they were chasing, and some of the more optimistic were already talking about shares of the prize-money from her capture.

It was common knowledge that since the British had concentrated more warcraft off the American coast, French ships had again taken to running the blockade from Gaudeloupe and Martinique with cargoes of rum, sugar and tobacco. If this should prove to be one of them, she might be a prize well worth taking.

All hands were called to breakfast early, so that the galley fires could be doused. When they swarmed back on deck once more the *Albatross* had gained enough to bring the stranger hull up —a scant league to leeward. They could guess at her size now. She was half again as big as the frigate, though her stubby masts carried no more canvas. Along her fat sides ran a broad white band, pierced for gun-ports. And at her main truck every now and then they could catch the flash of the tricolor flag.

Lieutenant Porter's marines were drawn up in formation on the quarterdeck and the captain, in all the glory of his dress uniform, was standing near the wheel, talking to his first officer. Jeff could hear his voice, not loud, but cool and drawling. "Very well, Mr. Cottington, you may beat to quarters. Call me when the bow-chasers are in range."

As the drummers began the long roll, he turned and went below, an elegant, unhurried figure.

Jeff sprang to his battle station with the rest and as orders began snapping from end to end of the ship, a whirlwind of activity began. Each gun captain told off his men to different tasks. One group brought up powder cartridges from the magazine. Another carried up solid shot and piled it in the chocks in the alleyway. Still others strewed handfuls of sand over the surface of the deck and rigged hoses to the pumps. The bulwarks were knocked down and the guns shotted and run out. The armorer, helped by half a dozen seamen, set out racks of cutlasses and boarding pikes at the foot of the mainmast.

Below, in the gun-deck, Jeff could hear the same preparations going forward. In fifteen minutes the men were standing at their guns. The ship was ready for battle.

With every inch of canvas drawing, the *Albatross* was swiftly overhauling the enemy. Only now and then could the men in the port side battery catch a glimpse of her over the frigate's bows, but when such a chance offered, Jeff was sure he could see tiny dots of men moving on the merchantman's deck.

The thudding report of a cannon came over the water, and the derisive cheer of the sailors forward indicated that the shot had fallen short.

"Just like they Frenchies," said a man at Jeff's side. "Too excitable to wait till they've 'alf a chance."

Several more minutes passed and then the deck quivered under them as one of their own long twelve-pounders in the bows was fired. The shot raised a white fountain right under the fleeing ship's counter.

Lieutenant Brown called one of the young midshipmen and sent him aft at a run. "Pass the word to Captain Frothingham," he said. "We've got the range with the bow guns now."

The twelve-pounders continued firing steadily, first one and then the other. As soon as the captain came on deck the frigate veered a point or two to starboard and moved down on the bigger ship's quarter.

Jeff heard a screaming sound overhead and saw a hole open suddenly in the fore-topsail. The Frenchman's nine-pounder stern gun had found the range at last, but the shot did little damage beyond tearing the sail and cutting a rope or two in the rigging.

Signal flags began to go up aboard the *Albatross*. MacGregor squinted aloft as the halyard carried them to the peak. "Yon's code for 'do ye surrender?'" he announced after a moment's study.

There was no answer from the French ship except a blast from one of her quarterdeck carronades. The heavy shot plumped into the waves a cable's length from the frigate's bow.

An order came from the quarterdeck and was relayed below. "Starboard gun-deck—ready a broadside. Wait till your guns bear!"

"That's Frothy for ye," clucked the Scotch gun-captain approvingly. "He'll come about an' gie her a rakin'."

Sure enough, within ten seconds the braces were hauled and the helm put over. At a distance of five hundred yards the *Albatross* flashed across the stern of the Frenchman, the long eighteens of the starboard battery thundering in quick succession as they were laid on the target.

Excitement brought a lump in Jeff's throat. He could feel the whole fabric of the ship shaking under his feet, and the acrid smell of burnt powder was thick in his nostrils. When the smoke of the broadside finally cleared he could see the big Frenchman wallowing along with battered stern-ports and mizzen topmast shot away. But it was on her deck that the worst havoc had been wrought. At that distance it looked as if half the crew were down, and the rest rushing in aimless circles.

Like lightning the *Albatross* backed her yards and came about. The men of the port battery raised a cheer. "Na then—it's our turn!" they yelled, and crowded ready by their gun-carriages.

But the carronades were still silent. Once more the frigate raked the enemy's stern with an eighteen-pounder broadside before squaring away for closer action. As they swept down along the Frenchman's starboard quarter the crew could see the frenzied activity aboard her. A crowd of sailors was hacking at the tangle of the mizzen rigging. Two officers struggled with the wheel, which had been half shot away. And through the open ports they caught glimpses of makeshift gun-crews straining at the tackles.

"Ready, port carronades!" shouted Lieutenant Brown. "Fire as you bear!"

MacGregor knelt at the breech of his gun,

gauging the elevation with his eye, twisting the screw a half turn. Forward, the bellowing report of the thirty-two pounders began.

"On the tackle, there!" MacGregor ordered and the men braced themselves against the recoil. As their carronade came abreast of the enemy's mainmast the Scot jerked at the lanyard and the huge gun leaped back with a deafening roar. Jeff's head was still ringing from the series of concussions as he helped run the carronade inboard and swab out its reeking barrel. They were just ready to load again when a sudden splintering crash threw them all to the deck.

Half dazed, Jeff struggled back on his feet. The next gun to theirs lay overturned, its oak slide smashed into kindling wood. Around it four of the crew were writhing in agony, and two others lay still in a widening pool of red.

The bo'sun's voice screamed in Jeff's ear. "Give a 'and, you! 'Elp get these 'ere wounded below!"

Shakily the boy lifted the twitching legs of the man who lay nearest, while another sailor took

THE HUGE GUN LEAPED BACK WITH A DEAF-
ENING ROAR

him by the shoulders. They staggered across the deck to the companion, waited for three powder-monkeys to bring up their loads, then made their way downward with as little jolting as possible. The wounded man was in terrible pain. He did not cry out but his breath came in choking gasps at every stride they took.

"This way, lads," called the surgeon, leading them down a second flight of steps into the gloom of the orlop deck. They laid the poor seaman down as gently as they could and hurried back to their stations, passing the other wounded men on the way.

Jeff's hands felt wet and sticky. He looked down at them with a shudder and wiped them hastily on his breeches. The overturned gun had been hauled back out of the way and sand had been scattered over the dark splotches on the deck. Except for that gaping hole in the line of carronades, the port battery was working as efficiently as if the fight were a daily drill.

A heavy pall of smoke still hung between the two ships, but from the sound of the Frenchman's spasmodic fire she seemed to be somewhere off the frigate's port quarter. Jeff took his place at the tackle rope and waited. A yell came from the lookout in the main top, and immediately the order was given to wear ship. Smartly the *Albatross* swung over to port. As the smoke eddied away they saw the bows of the enemy a bare hundred yards away and moving sluggishly nearer. Her canvas was shot to pieces, her rigging hanging in a loose tangle and her deck a shambles.

Captain Frothingham picked up his speaking trumpet.

"Strike!" his cold voice called. "Strike your colors or I'll have to rake you!"

The gunners stood tense, lanyards in their hands, as the ship's bowsprit loomed close. Then at last the shot-torn tricolor began descending. It caught on the down-haul for a second, jerked free and fluttered toward the deck, while a mighty cheer came from the crew of the frigate.

The hands sprang to the braces, the helm was thrown over, and they bore off just in time to avoid a collision.

Now that it was finished, Jeff felt a trembling all through his body. In the heat of the firing he had been too keyed up to be afraid. Even now fear had no part in his reaction. But when he remembered the white, tortured faces of the wounded men he felt a sickness at his stomach. He had been through a sea-fight and knew that he could face another one steadily. But as long as he lived he would never again look forward tc a battle as a lark.

CHAPTER VIII

NO SOONER had the French ship surrendered than all hands aboard the *Albatross* were piped aft and eighty men told off to man the cutter and the longboat. Jeff was assigned an oar in the cutter under Lieutenant Brown. They pulled away, cheering, and rowed over to the captured vessel while the frigate stood guard within easy range.

As they came up under the Frenchman's quarter, Jeff read her name: *"Ste. Elise,* Marseilles" —half the gilt chipped away and one of the "i's" dotted neatly by an eighteen-pound shot.

A French sailor with a bloody bandage around his head looked down at them dully and dropped a rope ladder. The lieutenant, followed by half the boat's crew, climbed rapidly to the ship's deck. It was a sorry spectacle that greeted them. All the guns but one or two were out of commission, the bulwarks shot through and through and the deck littered with splinters. Dead and wounded men lay in pitiful heaps in the scuppers. There was blood everywhere. Aloft the confusion was past imagining, for all three masts had suffered from the frigate's fire.

The twenty men still on their feet surrendered without a word and were sent over the side into the boats. The captain and first officer had both been killed by those first broadsides that raked the ship's stern.

Next the wounded were passed down for transfer to the frigate, and the sailmakers who had accompanied the boarding party set methodically about making canvas shrouds for the dead.

"Get at it, men," Lieutenant Brown ordered briskly. "We've got five hours of daylight to put her to rights. You, Durkin, send some hands aloft to see what they can do with that rigging. Never mind jury spars now. We can get enough sail on the main and foremasts to bring her into port."

Jeff was put to work with another squad cleaning up the decks, hacking away jagged splinters, righting guns and lashing tackle.

They drifted all afternoon with the frigate hove to, a cable's length off. Before the tropical sunset flared in the west, the *Ste. Elise* was ship-shape once more. With spare canvas set and a British jack run up to the main truck, the tired boarding party welcomed a prize crew aboard and rowed back to the man-o'-war. Then in the gathering dusk the two ships headed westward for Jamaica.

With light airs and a calm sea their voyage was slow. It was four days before the *Albatross* and her convoy sighted the mountainous Cuban coast and passed through the Windward Channel. In the meantime the crew had had time to repair most of the damage done in the fight. It was still a mystery how the gunners of a French merchant ship, after the battering they had received, could have aimed the shot that demolished the number six port carronade. " 'Twas na but a bit o' luck," MacGregor insisted. "An' verra bad luck for us. I couldna hae laid her better mysel'."

It was the morning of the sixth day after the battle when they hauled the yards and moved slowly into the roadstead of Kingston Harbor.

Between them and the town a score of ships lay at their moorings, and the blue water swarmed with market boats and lighters. Behind the white line of the buildings and the green plantations rose a ridge of mountains higher than any Jeff had ever seen. It had rained, early in the morning watch, but now the air was crystal clear, so that the hills fifty miles away stood out sharply against the sky.

The land looked very attractive to the young New Englander after his month at sea. He wondered hopefully if the crew would be given shore leave. No sooner had the frigate's anchor been dropped than a dozen small boats shot toward them, the Negroes at the oars whipping the water in a race to be first alongside. Two or three succeeded in getting close to the lower gun-ports before Durkin's bull voice warned them off, and from their loads of fruit they tossed up bananas and mangoes in return for the seamen's coppers.

Little Hammersley was one of the fortunate ones who caught a handful of fruit. As he successfully eluded the other midshipmen and darted up to the boat deck, he caught sight of Jeff.

"Come on," he cried, "I've got a treat!"

Together they ducked behind one of the forward carronades and squatted on a coil of rope to enjoy their feast. Hammersley handed Jeff something smooth and green that looked a little like a big pear. The Yankee examined it gingerly. His experience with tropical fruits extended only to bananas and oranges, and he had tasted them a bare half-dozen times.

"What do you do with it?" he asked.

"Peel off the rind, I should say, and see if the inside looks good to eat."

Jeff cut away the end with his clasp-knife and sniffed at the pulp. "Hmm," he said speculatively. "Sort of smells like turpentine."

"It's all right, I'm sure," the younger lad replied. "The people here just about live on them. They're called mangoes, I think. Wait—I'll taste it."

Between them they ate everything but the rind and the seeds, though the flavor was not quite as luscious as they had hoped. Sharing a big red-skinned banana was more enjoyable. Hammersley licked his lips and sighed when it was gone.

"A lot better than salt-horse and moldy biscuit," he said. "Maybe they'll get some fresh meat for the galley while we're here, too. I gave one of the hands tuppence for a fat rat the other day and it wasn't bad, stewed. But what I'd like to see is some real English mutton or a joint of beef!"

.   .   .   .

Jeff's hopes of getting ashore were doomed to disappointment. During the week the *Albatross* lay at anchor in the Jamaican port, the longboat and cutter were in constant use taking gay parties of sailors to Kingston, but none of the Americans were allowed off the ship. Day after day they pottered about the jobs assigned them by the bo'sun's mates. They scrubbed decks, tarred rope and polished brasswork, scurrying to cover under the awnings when the afternoon downpour struck the harbor. It was a monotonous life.

From young Hammersley, Jeff heard a glowing account of life in a tropical port, for the midshipman had had his wish gratified at last. With a full day ashore he had soon tired of the waterfront grogshops and gone off exploring outside the town. He told solemnly of a sugar plantation that stretched for miles along the road; of ram-

shackle old slave-quarters with as many inhabitants as an English market-town; of banana
plants so heavy with green fruit that their stalks
bent down at the top. More to the point, he
brought his friend a gift of juicy sugar-cane, cut
into short lengths and wrapped up in his hand-
kerchief.

To Jeff and the other Yankees the order to
weigh anchor was a welcome one. They were
tired of staring at a green shore they could not
reach. At least they would have real work to
keep them busy at sea, and they would be no
worse off than the rest of the crew. Jonas Beale
was out of the sick-bay now, his back nearly
healed of its cuts. He was thin and pale, and
though he limped about with a sullen look on
his face, the flogging had broken his spirit. He
offered no resistance to the gibes and blows that
came his way.

With Nate Winslow it was different. He kept
out of trouble, obeying orders quietly and
quickly, for he was as smart a seaman as any in
the ship. But there was a glint in his eye and a

set to his lean jaw that made Jeff uneasy. Sooner or later, under the constant irritation of navy discipline, he feared that the big Yankee's temper would flare.

There was one fellow aboard, a hulking, hard-faced bo'sun's mate named Scallon, who took a special delight in making life miserable for the Americans. He had cleverly knotted a piece of lead into the rope at the business end of his starter, and when he laid it on it bit like fire.

Nate and Jeff were spry enough to escape his blows for the most part, but he had a foul tongue and they had to take his insults in silence. As for poor Amos and Jonas Beale, their case was pitiable whenever the bully was on deck.

The *Albatross* had laid in such provisions as were to be had in Kingston, filled the casks with water, and replaced the ruined gun. She left the *Ste. Elise* in harbor to await the action of a prize court, and sailed off on a northeast slant for the Windward Passage. It was a month before the men aboard her sighted land again.

The strict routine of a man-o'-war made one

day pass very much like another. They ran through storms or lay rolling on an oily sea when no wind stirred. They practiced at the guns every afternoon, drilled at boarding and repelling boarders, learned to handle pikes and cutlasses. They were sent aloft to trim sail at the slightest pretext. Their spare time was employed in keeping the ship spick-and-span.

For a week the frigate cruised off the French West Indies, keeping a lookout for enemy ships, but all they sighted were a few small luggers and fishing-craft. Finally Capt. Frothingham turned her head northward and made for his old cruising ground off Bermuda.

They did not put in at Hamilton, however. The morning they expected to make their landfall, a sail came over the horizon and all hands were piped to quarters. Soon they could see it was a good-sized vessel, driving along under a press of sail.

"Deck, there!" came a call from the foretop. "I can see her colors, sir. She's British and a man-o'-war. From her rig I'd call her the *Pel-*

ican, sir."

At a distance of a mile or so the other frigate began signaling, and in a few minutes the captain ordered the crew of his gig called. Leaving Cottington in command of the deck, he went over the side in all the finery of his dress uniform and pulled smartly over to the other ship.

"Orders frae the Admiralty," MacGregor guessed. "Aiblin's it'll be guid news. They micht be sendin' us hame—or gie'in' us a double helpin' o' plum duff on Sunday."

They lay hove to and waited till well past noon. "Frothy'll be haein' his dinner in yon *Pelican's* cabin," the gunner winked. Sure enough, about six bells in the afternoon watch they saw the gig returning, the impeccable captain slouched in the stern sheets with his gold-laced hat cocked over one eye.

Two stiff-faced seamen helped him up the side and he made his way with great dignity to his cabin. His red, perspiring face bore witness to the quality of the *Pelican's* Madeira.

Evidently he had given a course to the first

lieutenant before retiring, for in a few moments the *Albatross* was squared away toward the northwest. They saw her sister frigate dip her colors and swing off on the opposite tack, heading back for Bermuda.

Jeff's excitement grew as they held the same course day after day. By his own reckoning they must be well up off the Virginia Capes and drawing nearer to the American coast every hour. One night on watch he had an opportunity to speak of it to Nate Winslow.

"You reckon we'll get close enough in to make a break for it?" he whispered.

"Not likely," Nate replied. "We'll be layin' off New York or Boston on blockade, I figger. If we git in sight o' land at all they'll keep an extra sharp watch on us. It'll be tough, though, to come that nigh an' not be able to do a thing about it."

The *Albatross* seemed to be in no hurry, whatever her destination. Even in fair weather she moved leisurely along under shortened sail. Once they sighted a distant ship and crowded on canvas to give chase. Within an hour, however, the lookout made the other craft out to be a British sloop-of-war—one of the eighteen-gun, brig-rigged vessels that had been used for years to harry commerce in the North Atlantic. After a brief interchange of signals she sailed off to the southward and the frigate resumed her course in the opposite direction.

It was an unusually fine, clear morning in June—the 10th of the month, according to the ship's calendar—when Jeff, up in the fore crosstrees, caught a glimpse of a low-lying shore to port. He had not been posted as a lookout and it was not his business to hail the deck. As soon as he finished his work on the yard, however, he looked around for Nate Winslow.

"I'd swear that was Cape Cod I saw," he told his big friend. Nate nodded. "Might be," he answered noncommittally. "More likely Nantucket, though. I got a squint at a light last night, that I figgered must be Block Island."

The frigate steered eastward all morning and in a few hours the hazy line of land had disappeared. That was the only sight Jeff was to have of his beloved New England for many a long day.

They voyaged slowly out across the gulf of Maine and the broad mouth of Fundy, bucked a northeast gale rounding Cape Sable and came to anchor in Halifax harbor on the 15th. There was no shore leave given. Captain Frothingham went into the town and was entertained for two days by the governor of the province. Then, without making his orders known, he had the crew weigh anchor again.

The course was southwestward now. They overhauled a Gloucester schooner inbound from the Banks, deep-laden with fish, and stopped her with a shot across her bows. Jeff raged at the sight of the cutter rowing over to board the unlucky craft. He knew too well how her crew would be browbeaten. When the marines returned they brought two husky young Gloucestermen with them—lads who had never been nearer England than the fishing grounds, but had been pressed as British seamen nevertheless.

Bewildered and unhappy, they looked around at the hostile, jeering faces and stumbled below with Scallon's rope's-end flicking at their backs.

Two days later, somewhere to the east of Sandy Hook, the lookout called the deck to report a sail. The vessel was coming fast, heading straight toward them with a good wind abeam.

"What's her rig? Can you make her out?" Lieutenant Cottington asked.

"Aye, aye, sir. It's the *Pelican,* sir, an' she's got a big hoist o' signals out."

A midshipman with the code book was sent into the foreshrouds at once. Jeff was near enough to hear every word as he read the flags and called the signals to the officer of the deck.

"It's not a regular code message, sir, except the start—'Urgent.' I'll have to spell it, sir. W-A-R—that's War. D-E-C-L-E—no, it's an A—R-E-D. War declared. B-Y, by—A-M-E-R-I-C-A-N, American. S-T-A-T-E-S. Got it, sir! They say War—"

But the first lieutenant was already racing

aft at top speed to carry the word to the cabin.

Jeff's heart suddenly felt too big for his chest. With a catch in his breath he turned to look for Amos and Nate.

CHAPTER IX

THE NEWS spread through the ship like a fire through dry grass. In five minutes there was not a man or boy aboard the *Albatross* who had not heard of the declaration of war. For the most part the crew greeted the idea with amusement. The brashness of a weak little nation like the United States in challenging mighty England was enough to raise a laugh.

While Jeff was still looking about for one of

his countrymen, the bo'sun's mate, Scallon, approached him. His small, mean eyes were half shut and his yellow teeth were bared in a leering grin.

"You bleedin' Yanks 'ave been arskin' fer trouble a long time," he told the boy gloatingly. "Now yer'll get it, an' plenty! 'Ow'll yer like it, w'en yer sees us sendin' the dirty little ships they call a navy to the bottom—eh? Turn yer 'and to a job o' work now, an' lively, or yer'll feel good British 'emp!"

The two frigates had hove to, a couple of cables' lengths apart, and a boat was put over the side in haste.

Captain Frothingham made his visit a short one, this time. Within half an hour he was back aboard, and the topmen were hurried aloft to make all sail. From high on the fore-royal yard Jeff watched anxiously to see what course they would take. He was half afraid the two ships might set off together for an immediate attack on one of the coast towns. In a moment, however, he was relieved to see the *Pelican* fill away to the northeastward. Down on the quarterdeck of the *Albatross* the wheel was put over, orders were given to haul the yards and taking the wind on her beam the vessel headed southeast.

Night had come before the boy had an opportunity to talk to Nate Winslow. He found the big sailor up in the bows, forward of the chaser guns. It was a secluded spot where no listener could approach them without being seen.

"What do you think, Nate?" Jeff whispered. "Is there going to be any fighting with the Americans?"

"I reckon so. They's some good men an' good ships in our navy, even if 'tain't very big. Might give 'em a surprise or two, 'fore this is over."

"What about us, then? They wouldn't make us work the guns against our own folks, would they?"

"I ain't sure. If they do, I aim to plain refuse an' take my floggin'. Wish to tunket I'd had sense enough to stay ashore, 'stead o' traipsin' off with ol' Cap'n Preble. I'd ha' been aboard the *Constitution* or the *President* by now, I guess.

We better not be seen talkin' together much from now on or they'll stick us in irons fer plottin' a mutiny."

There was plenty of work for all hands as the frigate crowded sail on the southward run. Discipline was enforced more strictly than ever, now that war had become a fact. The decks were kept cleared for action and double lookouts were on duty day and night. Whatever the new orders might be, the officers kept their own council. Not a man of the crew knew where they were bound.

For two days Jeff was half fearful—half hopeful—that they might sight a Yankee ship-of-war. Having seen something of the formidable character of British seamanship and gunnery, he dreaded having to watch them turned against his own flag. And yet a stubborn inner pride made him feel that the odds might not be too one-sided. If he should live through such a fight and the Yankees won—but that was almost more than he dared hope.

By the third morning they were a good four hundred miles to the southeast—somewhere on a line between Cape Hatteras and Bermuda, Jeff figured. It was a clear June day with a light, steady breeze blowing out of the northwest. The crew were exercising at the guns when a call from the foretop announced the discovery of a sail dead ahead.

The *Albatross* was already carrying royals. Now studding-sails were set, and every effort was made to overhaul the stranger. After a few moments it appeared that the other vessel had hove to, and was waiting to get a closer view of the frigate.

The gun-practice had been abandoned to handle the sails and now most of the crew lined the bulwarks, talking eagerly about the prospects of an encounter with the enemy. Soon the other craft was hull up to leeward.

"She's nowt but a brig-sloop," growled an old seaman standing near Jeff. "An' a little 'un at that. Might be our *Vixen,* sixteen guns. She's been on the Bahama station."

No flag had yet been shown at the smaller ship's maintop, but the confident way in which she awaited their approach seemed to indicate that she was British. They were less than two miles away now.

"Break out the colors," commanded Lieutenant Cottington, and the jack went fluttering aloft. Hardly had the halyards been made fast when they saw the sloop-of-war fall off the wind and fill away to the southwest. And at the same moment a rectangle of striped bunting whipped out at her masthead. It was the American flag. Jeff could hardly choke back the cheer that rose in his throat.

Actually no cheer of his would have been heard, for a yell went up from the whole crew at the sight. The pipes twittered frantically as all hands were called to quarters.

Without delay the frigate altered her course to starboard. Bowling along with the wind abeam she meant to keep the weather gauge as she overhauled her quarry. And when Jeff looked aloft at her tower of snowy canvas and heard the eager straining of her gear it seemed as if nothing on the sea could outstrip such a pursuit.

He had not counted on the fact that the little brig was both fast and smartly handled. She not only held her own but began to pull away. A trial shot from a long twelve in the frigate's bows fell short by several hundred yards, and a second ball, fired two or three minutes later, was still farther astern.

The *Albatross* hung on till noon, when she had fallen a full five miles behind, and at last gave up the chase. The sailors, itching for a fight, were grumbling as they trimmed the yards on the old course. Nate Winslow went past on some errand or other and gave his young friend a solemn wink. And when they slung their hammocks that night Jeff and Amos had a quiet chuckle over the impudent way in which the Yankee sloop had outfooted her more powerful enemy.

"I heard today," Amos whispered, "that they was g-g-goin' to put us in irons down in the c-c-cable tier if they got into action."

"Maybe they will," said Jeff. "I'd a blame sight rather be down there than have to fight a gun on the wrong side."

SHE BEGAN TO PULL AWAY

CLEAR FOR ACTION!

Next day they were in the middle of the Gulf
Stream and, though a trace of breeze still held,
the temperature on the open deck was almost
unbearable. There was no sparing the men because of the heat. They were kept at holystoning
the planking even when the pitch boiled in the
cracks. Jeff growled with the rest, but his lot was
far easier than that of the stocky Amos. Sweat
poured off the poor lad in rivers, and his good-
natured face was the color of a cooked beet.

When they were allowed to rest, the crew lay
panting under the scant shade of the awnings
and watched the strangely blue water slide past.
They were too hot and tired even to fish.

That afternoon the wind died completely. The
Albatross rocked sulkily on an oily swell and the
sun beat down without mercy. Four seamen who
had been kept at their tasks too long collapsed
from heat-stroke and had to be carried below to
the sick-bay. When the surgeon had made his
report to the quarterdeck the petty officers
stopped their driving tactics. The hands were
given a rest and an extra half-pint of water was

served out all around.

A little breeze sprang up after sunset and wind-sails were set to blow a draft into the gun-deck where the watch tossed in their hammocks. When Jeff was roused out at midnight he found the ship moving again. The cooling air was coming from the south now and the *Albatross* was close-hauled on the starboard tack.

It was slow going throughout the following day. Sometimes they lay becalmed and sweltering for hours at a time, and when there was wind it always seemed to blow from the wrong direction. The frigate beat laboriously back and forth, gaining a mile or two to windward for every ten she sailed.

Tempers grew short both forward and aft. The captain fumed and paced the quarterdeck, studying the weather signs. The mates and watch officers snapped at the men and the men quarreled among themselves. After one rumpus in the forward gun-deck half a dozen sailors lined up for inspection with black eyes and bashed noses. Lieutenant Cottington looked thoughtful as he passed down the line. He made no remarks to the combatants but that afternoon, after the regular ration of grog was passed out, he called out the ship's music.

"Jenks," he ordered, "get Williams up here with his fiddle, and old Tootles the fifer. Tell the men I'm putting up ten shillings and a plug o' Virginny tobacco to the fellow that dances the best jig."

The crew relaxed at once. Grumbling changed to cheers and laughter. No sooner had the fiddle and fife appeared than a wide ring was formed and the men crowded about, perching on the boats and gun-slides.

Williams was a long-nosed, solemn little Welshman from the frigate's galley. Reverently he unwrapped the faded blue cloth from his violin and cocked his ear to the strings while he tuned it. The fifer, a whiskered old cockney, lively as a cricket, was impatient to begin. He squeaked out a few bars of a quickstep and shuffled his feet on the deck. Some of the seamen took up the air, whistling and clapping their hands, and in a moment the strains of the fiddle joined in the tune.

Two sailors sprang out into the circle, jigging in a furious hornpipe. Their mates cheered them on, shouting for their favorites while the music played faster and faster. Two more men took their places as soon as they showed signs of tiring. For the better part of an hour the dance continued, till a score or more sailors had performed. Cottington and the other officers had been watching the contest from the quarterdeck. Now they called the names of three of the dancers whose efforts had brought the loudest applause, and these three stripped off their shirts, tightened their belts and settled down to battle it out in earnest.

They danced till old Tootles was scarlet in the face and the sweat flew off the Welsh fiddler like a shower of rain. At last one of the contestants dropped gasping on the deck, unable to take another step. One of the others was reeling and almost done. But the third—a tall, limber-legged Irishman with a grin like an ape and a devil in his eyes—pranced faster than ever. He leaped high in the air and kicked his heels together. He spun like a dervish, his soles beating the planking like a roll of drums.

When he was left alone in the ring the crew cheered as one man, so that the gulls that had perched in the frigate's upper rigging took fright and flew overhead in a screaming circle.

It was just as his mates were lifting the winner on their shoulders and the first lieutenant was taking a half sovereign from his pocket that the lookout hailed the deck.

"There's queer stuff floatin' 'ere, sir," he cried. "Looks like orange peel an' such."

Some of the officers and a crowd of seamen ran to look over the side. Around the ship they could see bright bits of flotsam. It was true—there were yellow rinds of oranges—banana skins—coconut husks.

"It must be the convoy, sir—the Jamaica fleet," one of the young midshipmen called to the quarterdeck. At once a lieutenant was sent into the shrouds with a glass, and as soon as he made his report, Captain Frothingham ordered the braces manned. The ship swung off to leeward and headed northeast with a stir of air on her quarter.

"What convoy are they talking about?" Jeff asked MacGregor, who was hauling with him on one of the weather braces.

" 'Tis the Jamaica ships, lad. A muckle fleet o' them sails out o' the Indies the last o' May. They were makkin' up when we put in at Kingston. The fleet's on its way to England the noo, and wi' a war started 'tis a fine prize they'd mak' for a Yankee squadron. Belikes old Frothy got his orders to convoy 'em when we spoke the *Pelican* last week."

They followed the scattered trail of fruit peelings for two days, with a freshening breeze pushing them along at a brisk clip. Extra lookouts were kept in the tops and the captain paced the afterdeck with his glass under his arm. Every few minutes he whipped it out to peer at the horizon, but Jeff noticed that the telescope was trained more often on the skyline astern or to the westward than on the sea ahead.

Late the second afternoon they met a British sloop-of-war beating southward for Bermuda and were told that she had sighted the convoy's stragglers early that morning.

"Look out for a squadron of American frigates!" the sloop's commanding officer yelled through his trumpet as the two craft separated. "They chased the *Belvidera* into Halifax a week ago!"

The *Albatross* dipped her colors and plowed forward in the wake of the merchant fleet. Captain Frothingham cocked an eye aloft and snapped an order to his first lieutenant before he went below. "Get more sail on her, Mr. Cottington," he said. "Royals and stuns'ls. Crowd on all she'll carry, and call me if you sight any ships before dark."

CHAPTER X

THE FRIGATE'S course to the northeast had carried her swiftly out of semi-tropic heat into the mists and cold that lay along the southern edge of the Grand Banks. Jeff felt the change as he lay in his hammock and he shivered when he was called on deck with the watch at midnight. The *Albatross* was rushing along through dark, heaving seas, the lookouts straining their eyes to see beyond those wraithlike wisps of fog.

That morning—it was the first day of July—dawned gray and cold. In the middle of the forenoon watch they sighted a small iceberg two or three miles off on the port bow. A "growler," the old hands called it. They explained that this was a piece that had broken off a larger berg, somewhere north along the Labrador, and was melting fast as it drifted into warmer waters. The fog had lifted temporarily. At seven bells, a half hour before noon, the forward lookout called the deck to report two sails, dead ahead, and a moment later he made out a third and a fourth. "It's the convoy!" he shouted. "I can see the cut of their canvas. Two full-rigged ships an' two brigs —an' there's more of 'em comin' in sight all the time."

"Good," said the captain. "We'll overhaul them in another two hours if this wind holds." With that he took his spyglass from the rack and went up the mizzen shrouds for a long look astern. When he came down he ordered the decks kept cleared for action and all hands at their posts.

Involuntarily Jeff stared at the sea to windward but from where he stood on the deck there was no sign of a sail in the gray haze that shrouded the horizon. Something must have happened to delay the Yankee squadron. If they had been off Halifax the week before and knew of the convoy's movements, they should have had ample time to come up with it.

The *Albatross,* under full canvas, continued to gain on the merchantmen. Half a dozen of them were now in plain view. They were deep-laden, clumsy craft, lumbering along with too few sails and crews too small to handle them.

At their first glimpse of the onrushing frigate, some of the ships showed signs of scattering like hens before a hawk. Then the big British flag came into view and they clawed back into their huddle once more.

The wind had been fading for an hour. Just as the *Albatross* hauled abreast of the last straggler in the fleet, a bank of fog crept down from the north and they could no longer see each other.

CLEAR FOR ACTION!

"Get to the bell, there!" ordered Lieutenant Cottington. "Keep it sounding—six strokes to the minute." A hollow clang from the big fog-bell went shuddering out into the mist, and was repeated each ten seconds as the bo'sun counted off the time. Meanwhile other bells began to sound through the gray fog curtain. Some were close at hand and clear, others faint and muffled by distance. So they drifted all afternoon.

Once the spars of a good-sized brig loomed up, ghostly, a scant fifty yards from the frigate's quarter. There were shouts and an exchange of names and greetings. More than forty ships had started from Kingston together, the brig's skipper informed them. But they had been separated by a storm and several craft had put back after developing leaks. There was a sloop-of-war somewhere ahead, he thought. No, they had seen nothing of any Yankee vessels, and this was his first news that war had actually been declared.

Soon the brig sheered off and was swallowed in the fog. After that they knew of her presence only by the doleful sound of her bell.

That cruise across the North Atlantic was a strange, nightmarish business. Jeff never seemed to get enough sleep, for the watches were often interrupted. Matching her pace to the plodding merchantmen, the *Albatross* moved always under shortened sail, and on days when the fog lifted she was constantly making hurried sorties to round up some straying member of the convoy. These merchant captains, Jeff thought, were like a flock of silly sheep, straggling off when they should have sense enough to stick together. The frigate snapped at their heels, herding them along for all the world like Squire Deering's collie dog, back in the pasture at Shinnequid.

Every day he woke expecting to hear the guns of pursuing American men-of-war, and every night he went to his hammock disappointed. What a chance they were missing! What havoc a few fast-sailing frigates could have played in this unwieldy mass of ships, most of them un-armed, guarded only by the *Albatross* and one smaller vessel! He had no way of knowing that at that moment Commodore Rodgers' squadron was hardly more than a day's sailing to the westward, hunting through the fog for some trace of the West Indian fleet.

It was two full weeks from the time the frigate had come up with the convoy to the afternoon they sighted land at the entrance of the English Channel. The day was gray and blowy, with clouds racing in from the west and a strong sea running.

Little Hammersley, the midshipman, came to stand beside Jeff. "Look!" he pointed exultantly. "That white line of surf—see it? That's the Lizard! It's Cornwall! It's England! Maybe I'll be home on leave before the week's out!"

Jeff looked from the distant pinpoint of surf to the youngster's shining eyes and felt a stab of homesickness for the rocky coast of his own land. "I hope you're right, sir," he said and turned away so that the boy would not see his face.

But there was no shore-leave waiting for the men of the *Albatross*. The news of the fleet's approach brought two big line-of-battle ships out of Plymouth the next morning. They rolled majestically down on the rear of the convoy, their towering canvas and triple tiers of guns glinting in the sun.

Signal flags were run up aboard the nearer of the two, and for an hour messages were passing between her and the *Albatross*. A few of the frigate's hands knew enough of the code to get the sense of what was being said. Their faces grew long as they read the flags, and the word went swiftly through the ship that they were not to land. The three-deckers would take over their convoy duty and see the merchant fleet into the Thames. Captain Frothingham's orders were to turn back at once and sail for the West Indies station by way of the Azores.

The temper of the crew was sullen that noon as they hauled the yards, brought the ship about and began the long beat down the Channel. Off there to starboard, scarcely a league away, they could see the green headlands of England flecked with sun and chasing cloud shadows. They could see little towns nestling under the cliffs—red-roofed cottages and cozy taverns—the masts of fishing boats, snugged down in safe harbors. All the call of the land was there, reaching out for sailors weary of the sea.

The mates and petty officers were no happier than the men, but at least they had an outlet for their feelings. They drove the hands with such scowling ferocity that no member of the crew had a moment to sulk.

It was no particular disappointment to Jeff and his fellow Americans that the new orders sent the *Albatross* back to her cruising without touching land. Nevertheless, they had to suffer under the same harsh discipline as the rest. If anything their misery was greater, for a fresh hostility toward Yankees was making itself felt throughout the ship.

Jeff caught a hint of it in the way young Hammersley tried to avoid him. MacGregor, too, was grumpy and unfriendly. And the bully Scallon took a savage delight in singling out the American sailors and forcing them to do the dirtiest jobs he could find.

They pounded slowly west by south through battering head seas and at last, one blowy morning, the lookout sighted the black, surf-beaten rocks of Ushant. Captain Frothingham seemed to be in no hurry to haul away from the hostile French coast. He ordered the helm put down and cruised to leeward under shortened sail, as if in his present mood he would welcome a fight with any craft that dared stir out of Brest or St. Nazaire.

But no sail showed itself. At the end of a day of prowling within sight of the coast, the frigate shaped a course across the windy Bay of Biscay for Cape Finisterre. The breeze, which had been westerly for a week, shifted to the northwest in the night and made their progress easier. Now that it was no longer necessary to tack ship every few minutes the crew had time to rest. Their discontent had been pretty well sweated out of them. But although Jeff heard less complaining among the watch below, he found the feeling against himself and the other Yankees was as bitter as ever. In some way they seemed to be held personally responsible for the fact that their countrymen had started a war—and that the war had killed the chances of shore leave.

Two days of good sailing weather with the wind abeam saw them well past the Spanish Cape and running on a southwesterly slant toward the Azores. Then one night when Jeff's watch was on deck, the stars began to disappear one by one and the wind freshened in strong gusts from the north. In five minutes the sky was completely obscured. A black mist whirled across the decks, shrouding the frigate's rigging and throwing a moist halo about her running lights. She was racing through the waves now, plunging and straining at her cordage. Lieutenant Brown gave an order and the hands were piped aloft to shorten sail.

Jeff found the topgallant yard slippery with the drenching mist and swaying perilously to the pitching of the ship. In the inky darkness they fumbled for the sail and finally succeeded in furling its wet bulk in the gaskets. Amos Gilman was next to Jeff on the foot-rope. The big youngster shivered as they groped their way back to the mast.

"G-g-golly, I'm cold," he said. "Soaked to the s-s-skin, I be!"

He hesitated, with one hand on the shrouds, and suddenly gripped his friend's arm. "Look!" he gasped. "A l-l-light!"

Jeff stared into the swirling mist. "Where?" he asked.

" 'Twas right off there." The boy pointed to starboard. "Jest fer a s-s-second I seen it. Now it's gone!"

Jeff put an arm around his companion's broad back and felt him shaking. "Here," he said sharply, "you've got to get below. You're seeing things!"

"No—I tell ye it was there," Amos protested, but Jeff pushed him firmly downward. He was worried about his friend. The damp and chill must have brought on a fever, he thought, for it was certain that no ship's lantern could be seen half a cable's length away in that driving fog.

When the watch changed he saw Amos safely

into his hammock and laid his own jacket over him, tucking it in with care. "How do you feel now?" he asked anxiously.

"Hey—listen," the other boy replied with some vehemence, "I ain't sick. There *was* a light there—honest. S-s-sort of a glow, like. I know it sounds c-c-crazy, but I seen it."

He flopped over with his back to his unbelieving chum, and was soon snoring. Jeff couldn't get to sleep immediately, for the matter still bothered him. He had heard strange stories of phantom ships that appeared in storms at sea. He had seen the tricks played by phosphorescent patches on the waves and the queer thing sailors called St. Elmo's fire that glowed sometimes at the tip of a spar in thundery weather. And yet as Amos had told it, this sounded like none of them. Could it be possible that, rushing along at a round ten knots as they were, they had passed within a few yards of another vessel—passed without a hail from either ship's lookout? The whole idea was fantastic. He yawned once and snuggled down comfortably in his hammock.

And his next conscious thought was when he struggled awake at the sharp note of the bo'sun's pipe four hours later.

Amos Gilman seemed healthy enough that wet, blowy morning. He grinned at Jeff and gave him a playful shove as they started up the ladder. On deck the mist was still too thick to see far over the tall gray seas. And even under reefed topsails the frigate plunged along giddily with a screaming wind on her quarter. Hand-ropes had been stretched along the gangway between the guns. Several times that morning Jeff had to grab at them to save himself when he was hurrying to obey an order.

It was nearing noon, and the watch on deck was waiting for eight bells to strike, when the lookout in the main shrouds gave a sudden shout. His words were carried away by a gust of wind but there was no mistaking his excitement, or the urgent gesture of his pointing arm.

Right abeam and hardly a hundred yards off, the amazed crew saw the top-hamper of a ship looming through the smother. She was running on a parallel course and in the same direction as the *Albatross.* And streaming from her main truck was the tattered tricolor flag of France. Lieutenant Brown gave a sharp order to the quartermaster at the wheel and sent a scared midshipman diving into the cabin companion to call out the captain. In an instant the ship was echoing to the crackle of commands, the furious shrilling of pipes and the thud of running feet.

"Stations, there! . . . Call all hands. . . . Ready starboard guns. . . . Tubs on deck and light your matches!"

In spite of what looked like hopeless confusion, the gun crews went to work grimly and efficiently. In two minutes every carronade in the starboard battery was loaded, primed and run out. The port-side crews, Jeff among them, were told off to carry powder and shot. One gang brought up tubs of sand and bundles of slow-match, lighted at the galley stove, for in the wet weather flintlock firing was bound to be uncertain.

The French ship meanwhile had sheered off

only a point or two and was forging slightly ahead. She was clearly visible through occasional gaps in the wall of mist—a big, black frigate with a double row of gun-ports and a yelling crew swarming on her decks.

The men of the *Albatross* worked frantically with handspikes and tackle to slew the after guns around so that they would bear. But with the weather gauge the Frenchman was pulling steadily ahead.

"Ready with your matches!" roared Brown. "Forward guns—let 'em have it at the word!" He lifted his arm, waiting for the roll of the ship, but before he could bring it down a shattering crash shook the timbers under their feet. The French frigate had sent a point-blank broadside into the starboard bow.

CHAPTER XI

AT THAT range and with the weight of metal it carried, the effect of the Frenchman's broadside was terrible to behold. It tore a huge breach in the forward bulwark, put two carronades out of action, ripped the fore-course to shreds, and left the forecastle strewn with dead and wounded.

But in the rest of the ship the iron discipline of the British Navy kept every man at his station. Lieutenant Brown did not move a step. He waited a bare second for the downward roll and dropped his arm. "Fire!"

All the guns that were still in commission and bearing on the enemy's hull roared in unison.

"Man the braces!" came the captain's clear cry. "Back topsails, ready to come about! Port battery, there—stand to your guns!"

The gun-crews, Jeff's included, sprang to their work like tigers. In a matter of seconds they had sweated the guns back, rammed home the powder charge, double shot and wadding, poured fresh priming and run the carriages out again. MacGregor stood coolly by the butt of his cannon, blowing on the red tip of his slow-match. "All steady, there," he growled to his men. "It maun be a meenit till she bears. But lose nae time on the tackle, when I gie ye the word."

The men hauling the yards carried out their maneuver like lightning. Hardly had the other frigate's stern cleared their bowsprit when the helm was thrown hard over and the *Albatross* swung sharply up to starboard. A pair of brass chasers in the Frenchman's stern-ports began barking. Then they saw that she too was coming into the wind, her crew hauling desperately to bring her broadside on before she could be raked. But already she was blanketed by the sails of the *Albatross*. Staring through the aperture beside the gun, Jeff could see her lofty poop a bare biscuit-toss away—the gunners swabbing the brass six-pounders—the officers waving their arms in wild gesticulations.

Aboard both ships the crackle of musketry was almost continuous now, and the balls rattled like hail in the rigging. Jeff waited, holding his breath, as the Scotchman sighted along his piece.

"Fire as you bear," came the lieutenant's order, and somewhere forward the guns began to bellow.

" 'Ere's one fer old Boney!" yelled the captain of the next carronade, laying his match to the powder. And then it was their turn. The deck shook to the deafening *boom* of the big gun and the men on the tackle were nearly jerked off their feet by the recoil.

For the next few moments the gun-crews were too breathlessly busy even to glance at the enemy. It was only when the carronades had been reloaded and run out that Jeff had time to look around. The musket fire had strangely ceased, and except for shouted orders and the groans of wounded men, the heaving deck was quiet. The boy saw that the frigate had once more fallen off the wind and was bowling along with half a gale on her quarter. The white streamers of mist that blew past were thicker than before. He looked vainly about for the enemy ship.

"What's happened? Where'd she get to?" he asked the man next him in bewilderment.

"We're a-chasin' of 'er now," the sailor replied. "Arter that last broadside she kept 'fore the wind an' run off in the mist whiles we was slackin' the sheets. Jus' disappeared, she did!"

The *Albatross* ran southerly for two hours, her lookouts peering eagerly into the fog for a glimpse of the Frenchman. Durkin, the bo'sun, was fuming. " 'Tain't right nor nat'ral," he growled. "We 'ad 'er 'ulled proper, an' 'alf 'er riggin' shot away. Another broadside or two an' she'd 'a' struck 'er colors. This blarsted fog is wot saved 'er."

It was beginning to grow dark when the frigate abandoned the chase and hauled away westward. The men were disappointed. It wasn't in the bulldog tradition of His Majesty's service to lose an enemy once they had got their teeth in her. But hunting for a ship in that welter of mist was like a search for a needle in a haystack.

A carpenters' crew had spent the late afternoon patching up the damage in the frigate's bows as best they could. The Frenchman had evidently mounted forty-two pounders on her carronade deck, for one of the huge balls was brought up from below and exhibited. It had plowed through the thick oak planking close to the waterline and wrecked a part of the forward hold. Half the water-casks were stove in and some of those that were left had their staves started so that they were leaking.

The ship's carpenter and his helpers soon had

a spare sail stretched over the hole in the hull and applied a jury patch to the inside. By nightfall the men at the pumps reported that the level of water in the well was no longer rising. They were keeping ahead of the leak.

That night on watch, with the wind still howling through the shrouds, Amos Gilman reminded Jeff of the phantom light he had seen. "Thought I was sick or crazy, didn't ye?" he chuckled. "There was a light, right enough—an' it was aboard that Frenchy. We must have been runnin' along with her like a t-t-team o' hosses all night."

At noon the next day sea-burial was given the four men who had been killed in the fight. Lined up in the gangway, the crew stood at sober attention while the brief service was read and the long, sail-cloth-covered bundles tilted over the side. Of the wounded, below in the orlop deck, three had lost legs or arms by amputation and one other was likely to die from the effect of a splinter through his lung. The brief engagement with the French frigate had been a costly one.

But the injury that had been done to the supply of fresh water seemed to worry the officers even more than the loss of men or the damage to guns and hull. Rations were cut to two pints a day and the cooper was put to work tightening barrels and cutting staves for new ones. The word went through the ship that they would put in at the Azores for water and supplies.

Jeff mentioned this report to Nate Winslow when he had a chance to talk to him alone. "How far you reckon it is to the Azores?" he asked eagerly.

" 'Twon't take no more'n three or four days to git there if this wind keeps up," the big sailor answered. "But don't set too much store by them islands, lad. I know what you're thinkin'—a chance to git away in a neutral port. But, shucks! Horta might as well be England, they's so many British men-o'-war puts in there."

"You've seen the islands, Nate?"

"Yeah, I was ashore there off a whaler once. It's a pretty enough place. Tall hills an' orange groves—plenty o' rain an' sun to make things grow. But the folks ain't very good company. Mostly Portygee an' such, with a lingo no Maine man can understand."

Jeff's hopes were not entirely dashed by his friend's words. The islands sounded like a pleasant place, and who could tell whether some chance for escape might not offer when it was least expected?

But as it turned out, all he saw of the Azores was the shadowy loom of a mountain peak between sea and sky at dawn of the fourth morning. The mist had cleared the day before, but the wind came blustering out of the north with as much force as ever.

Hardly had they made their landfall when another call came from the lookout in the main top. "Sail, ho!" he yelled. "Full-rigged ship to leeward. There's another—and another—I count five sail in all, sir!"

As the light grew they were visible from the deck. Three big ships and two smaller ones, cruising together on a line that would cut the frigate's course if she stood in for the islands.

CLEAR FOR ACTION!

"What do you make them?" shouted the officer of the deck.

"Nearest one's a two-decker, sir. Can't make out her ensign without a glass."

Lieutenant Brown hurried up the mizzen shrouds, telescope in hand. After a long look he came down again even faster and ducked into the cabin. Jeff could see that three ships of the squadron had hauled closer to the wind and were now rapidly approaching the *Albatross*. The next moment the captain appeared on the quarterdeck and began snapping out commands.

To most of the crew, who had taken it for granted that the fleet was British, the order to clear for action came as a surprise. At the same time the helm was put over and the yards trimmed. The frigate was going to keep up to windward and run for it.

Standing by his gun, Jeff stared at the leader of the pursuing ships. Suddenly he choked back an exclamation. At her masthead flew the flag of his own country! Five armed vessels—this must be the same American squadron that had been hunting the West Indian convoy in the fog on the Banks. Had they followed clear across the Atlantic?

Even while the decks were being readied for action, a gang of topmen had been sent aloft to set more sail. The royals were drawing now, and the frigate bowed far over to the force of the wind, scudding through the green seas like a race-horse.

Scallon, the surly bo'sun's mate, came hurrying up and caught Jeff by the arm. "Come on wi' me," he growled. "I've orders to stick all you misbegotten Yankees below in the brig."

Brandishing his starter threateningly, he drove the American seamen down the hatch and crowded them into a small, foul compartment of the forward hold. When they were all inside they heard the key turn in the padlock, and Scallon tramped away.

There were six of them there in the semi-darkness—the four who had been taken off the *Abigail* and the two young Gloucester fishermen, pressed a few weeks later. Jonas Beale crouched in a corner, his face pale and drawn and his body shaking.

"What are they goin' to do to us?" he snarled. "How long do we stay in this stinkin' hole?"

"Till the fight's over, I reckon," Nate Winslow answered calmly. "Mebbe we'll be sunk, or blown to glory. Mebbe we'll be captured, an' have a chance to serve in our own navy. Then again there's no sayin' they can catch us. Anyhow, there ain't a thing to do right now but rest easy an' hope fer the best."

For ten minutes no sound reached the ears of the prisoners except the creaking and groaning of timbers and the squeak of rats. Then from a long way off came the thudding *boom* of a cannon.

"They've opened fire," said Nate. "Don't sound to me like they was in range, though."

The sound was repeated from time to time but it never seemed to come any nearer. Then they heard a sharper, jarring report, close at hand. For a moment Jeff thought one of the American frigates had come up with them, but he soon realized that it was the *Albatross* trying the range with one of her long nines, mounted in the stern.

The deck under their feet continued to tilt to port. That meant that the frigate had not been forced to come about. She was holding her lead and making a westward reach of it, with the wind barely forward of her beam.

The day dragged by with no further attention paid to the six Yankees. The Gloucester boys moped unhappily, Amos snoozed on a coil of rope and Jonas Beale continued to swear and fidget. Finally Nate spoke to him sharply. "Quit playin' baby," he said. "Ain't a mite o' good cussin' the luck. We're here, an' we'll stay here a spell, so pull yerself together an' act like a real sailor."

They had been shoved below without breakfast. Now, with the passage of hours, Jeff began to be not only hungry but very thirsty. "You reckon they plan to starve us?" he asked Nate.

"They been too busy to bother about us," the big seaman replied. "Dry, are ye? Me, too. But don't count on much water fer a spell. Now we've been chased off from the Azores it'll be another thousand miles 'fore we can fill the casks."

The sound of firing had finally died away altogether, but the frigate was still on the same course, heeled down to leeward, her timbers complaining under the drive of the sail she carried. What little light had come in through cracks in the bulkhead now gradually faded, and they sat in pitch darkness. They could hear the bell struck, faintly, and the pipes calling a change of watch. At last Jeff was roused from uncomfortable dreams by the grating of the key in the lock.

"Tumble out here, ye lubbers," came Scallon's harsh voice, and blinking in the light of the lantern he carried, they made their way to the deck. Durkin was waiting there for them.

"Bear a hand at the braces," he croaked. The wind had shifted slightly and the watch was trimming the yards. There was no sign of a pursuing fleet anywhere on the dark horizon. Much as Jeff wondered what had become of the American ships, he knew no questions would be answered by the hostile British crew, so he kept silent and stuck doggedly at his work.

It was midnight before he tasted food or drink. Then, when he went below at eight bells, he was given a single ship's biscuit and a pannikin of water. The scummy liquid was hardly enough to wet his parched throat, but it did him no good to ask for more. The petty officer in charge scowled at him angrily. "We're all on short rations," was his gruff answer. "An' why? It's because o' them blarsted Yankees as kept us out o' Horta. If I was old Frothy I'd have ye in irons fer the rest o' the v'yage!"

There was little to relieve the boy's black discouragement as he crawled into his hammock that night. The *Albatross* had outsailed the American frigates. Until that moment he had not realized how heavily he had counted on deliverance from that quarter. And the chase had served to heighten the ugly feeling of the crew toward him and his fellows. From now on they could expect a still greater share of kicks and curses. But weary, starved and desperate as he was at that moment, Jeff clung fiercely to one hope. Somehow, no matter what it cost him, he meant to make his escape from the ship.

CHAPTER XII

SHORT of water as they were, the officers of the *Albatross* seemed to have no intention of putting back to the Azores. All through the following day the frigate beat to the westward. Then, as no sail had been sighted, she fell off on a southerly slant, hoping to pick up the northeast trades. There were several days of uncertain weather when sultry calms were succeeded by thunder squalls. But at last, drifting south past the thirtieth parallel, they found a steady wind blowing out of the east.

That voyage across the Atlantic never seemed quite real to Jeff when he looked back on it afterward. There was a dreamlike monotony about it. Every day the light breeze held and the ship logged her hundred and twenty miles with scarcely a hand laid to the ropes. The heat, the hard glitter of the sea, the everlasting drills and the drudgery of deck-work went on without variation. And each morning and night the water was doled out sparingly to men who had grown sullen with thirst. Once or twice sailors were caught trying to steal a drink and flogged with the cat as an example to the rest of the crew.

Below in his hammock Jeff dreamed sometimes of deep, bubbling fountains of clear water —of spring freshets in Shinnequid River, when icy streams came tumbling down out of the hills. He woke from such a dream one morning, a fortnight after they had sighted the Azores, and lay for a while, blinking up at the deck-beams. His mouth tasted dry and cottony and his stomach felt hollow under his ribs. A moment before he had been drinking his fill from a bucket that brimmed with clear, cold well-water. Why couldn't he have stayed asleep?

Just then he heard a sharp hail somewhere above and a thud of running feet. Excited voices came down to him. It was barely daylight, and the watch still had two hours below decks, but he was no longer sleepy. Pulling on his breeches he hurried up the ladder.

All hands were crowded forward, staring at something out there across the purple sea. Jeff jumped into the fore shrouds and looked in the same direction. Above the shadowy horizon jutted a dark peak, its summit touched with rosy light by the rising sun.

From the quarterdeck Lieutenant Cottington studied the island through his glass and ordered the helm put over so that their course lay straight for it. During the next two hours the crew watched fascinated while the mountain grew and the land took form. They could see a thin white line of surf breaking on an outer reef, and within its circle a dark volcanic cone that lifted steeply out of green jungle to a height of two or three thousand feet.

Nobody seemed to know what the name of the island might be. If it was on the charts, the officers kept its identity to themselves. Some of the crew swore they had seen it before and one or two thought they could even remember the entrance through the reef and the anchorage inside. The general opinion was that the island lay by itself, somewhere a day's sail or more to the east of the Windward chain.

When they were within three or four miles the order was given to take in canvas. The *Albatross* crept slowly toward the outer barrier with double lookouts posted and a leadsman in the bow chains constantly calling soundings. Cautiously they skirted the reef to the northward until an opening in the surf several hundred yards wide showed them a clear passage. Then a boat was lowered and Lieutenant Brown went through with a picked crew of rowers, taking soundings while the ship lay hove to outside.

Finally they saw the lieutenant stand up in the stern-sheets and wave a signal.

As soon as the yards were trimmed the frigate made a short tack to bring her abreast of the pass and slipped through into the lagoon as neatly as if she were maneuvering to an anchorage in her home port. Jeff joined in the spontaneous cheering of the crew. He felt oddly excited. Amos was there on deck but he looked about in vain for Nate Winslow. He wanted desperately to have a word with the big Maine man.

There was no opportunity to search for his friend just then, for no sooner had the *Albatross* dropped anchor than the hands were ordered to hoist water casks out of the hold. It was hard, hurrying work with the tropic sun blazing down on deck and the bo'sun's mates driving the men with their rope's-ends.

At last the barrels were all on deck and the cutter and longboat were swung out. Jeff listened eagerly as Durkin told off the crews to man them. As he and Amos took their places in the cutter he craned his neck for a glimpse of

Nate Winslow, but apparently the tall Yankee had not been assigned an oar. They loaded half a dozen casks amidships and started pulling for the beach.

Inside the barrier reef the lagoon lay clear and blue, with pleasant little waves ruffling to the breeze. Seabirds circled overhead, complaining shrilly at this invasion of their private fishing ground. It took only two or three minutes of rowing to bring the cutter into shoal water, and as the order came to ship oars Jeff looked up into the green shadow of a mangrove thicket. The rank stems rose out of the tide in an impenetrable mass on the left of the boat. On the right there was a beach of pinkish sand that extended fifty or sixty yards before the mangroves began again.

Barelegged, the crew jumped over the side and ran the nose of the boat up on the sand.

"This way—and bring your barrels," came a hail from Lieutenant Brown.

Jeff and Amos lifted one of the big casks over the gunwale and began rolling it in the direction of the voice. There were other seamen ahead of them and behind them, all joking and skylarking at the feel of land under their toes.

"Gosh!" murmured Amos. "L-l-lookit, Jeff—palm trees! An' p-p-parrots!"

The path they were following ran upward between giant green ferns, skirting the mossy edge of a rivulet. Above their heads the fronds of coconut palms made a constant, cool, rustling murmur. And bright-plumaged birds darted through the leaves with queer, raucous cries.

The procession of sailors moved along the path for nearly a hundred yards before they overtook the scouting party. In a glade among the palms they saw Lieutenant Brown's men kneeling beside a deep, clear pool, laughing and sputtering as they dipped their faces in the cool water. From a ledge of dark rock overhanging the hollow gushed a bright cascade—a living spring that fed the pool and the little stream below.

One after another the seamen dropped their barrels and rushed forward. After his first deep drink Jeff pinched himself to make sure he wasn't dreaming again, for the beauty of the fountain and the sweet, cold taste of its water were all he had imagined and more.

The men of the *Albatross*—leather-faced old sea-dogs and reckless youngsters alike—laughed and chattered like children let out of school. One burly topman, carried away by the thrill of the moment, plunged his bare legs knee-deep into the pool. In an instant Scallon's lead-weighted starter seared his ribs.

" 'Ere, you!" yelled the hulking bo'sun's mate. "Keep yer dirty 'ide out o' that water! Want to poison the lot of us?"

Lieutenant Brown stepped forward. "That's enough, men," he ordered sharply. "You've had your drink. Now get at it. Start filling those casks."

It was a long afternoon's work. As soon as a barrel was filled and the bung driven home, a pair of sailors rolled it laboriously down the path to the beach. It took the combined strength of half a dozen men to heave the cask into the cutter. Then, when the boat was loaded so deeply that her gunwales were almost awash, she was rowed out to the anchored man-o'-war.

An arrangement of slings and tackle had been rigged from the gun-deck to hoist the water barrels inboard. At each trip he made to the frigate, Jeff looked about for Nate Winslow, but his friend was nowhere in sight. He must have been sent below, the boy decided, to help stow the barrels in the hold.

A wild plan was beginning to take shape in Jeff's mind. It had been there, he realized, from the moment he had sighted the island that morning. Through the day he had hardly dared to think about it seriously, but with sunset drawing near and the last of the barrels about to be filled, he knew it was now or never.

Earlier in the day a squad of red-coated marines had been brought ashore to stand guard. For hours they had tramped the beach and the path leading to the pool, sweltering under the weight of their muskets and equipment. Now, with the work nearly finished, their vigilance was

IT WAS A LONG AFTERNOON'S WORK

relaxed. Some of them had slung off their knap-sacks and jackets and were sitting under the palm trees mopping their sunburned faces.

As Jeff and Amos went up the path for the last time they heard a thud of running feet behind them. Jonas Beale appeared suddenly from around a bank of ferns. There was a crazy look in his eyes and the sweat was pouring off his face. He seized Jeff's arm and spoke in a choking whisper.

"I'm goin' to make a break for it!" he panted. "Come on—they'll never catch us. I got a place picked in them thick bushes down by the shore!"

"When?" Jeff asked.

"Right now!" Beale urged hoarsely. "Nobody'll see us!"

The boy hesitated a second. He too had been thinking about escape, but he had planned it differently. Then he heard footsteps coming down the path.

"Wait!" he whispered. But the Yankee seaman had already darted into the green wall at the right of the trail.

Jeff thought fast. "Come on, Amos—act natural!" he breathed, and led the way forward as if nothing had happened. Before they had advanced five paces the twisting path brought them face to face with Durkin and Scallon.

"Look lively, there," the bo'sun growled at them. "Don't keep the cutter waitin'."

As they passed, his evil-faced companion turned as if to follow the two lads, but at that moment there were shouts from the direction of the beach. A musket banged loudly, sending the birds up from the trees in a frightened rush.

"Wot's that?" Scallon demanded in a startled voice.

"It's trouble," snapped Durkin. "Don't stand there, ye big lout! Come wi' me!" And he began to run down the path at a lumbering trot.

The instant they were out of sight Jeff grabbed the bewildered Amos by the wrist. "Quick!" he whispered. "We'll go this way. Watch you don't leave a track!"

He jumped as high as he could, to clear the thick green tops of the ferns on the left, and dove under a tangle of hanging vines beyond. The vegetation grew so thick that he was almost smothered as he plunged through it. He was bent double, his eyes closed against the constant swish of leaves, his hands out before him like a swimmer's, parting the foliage.

Jeff didn't dare stop or even look behind him, but he could hear Amos puffing at his heels. Whatever it was that had caused the shouting and firing, the attention of the crew had been distracted for the moment at least. He was certain nobody had seen them leave the path, and with luck it might be four or five minutes before their absence was discovered.

When his breath was gone he crouched in the semi-darkness under a broad-leaved plant and waited till the other boy joined him.

"Listen!" he cautioned, as Amos sank down exhausted at his side. In the distance he could hear faint sounds of shouting again, and then, unmistakably clear, another musket-shot.

"I'm afraid it's Jonas," he panted. "They must be chasing him—like they'll be chasing us pretty quick."

He looked into the other lad's fat, good-natured face and felt a qualm of conscience. "Amos," he said, "I got you into this without telling you anything beforehand. After Jonas made his try, it looked like our only chance. But I've got to say it now. We're deserters. If they catch us, it's all up. Either we'll be shot out o' hand or dragged back to the ship an' given a thousand lashes—a lot worse than shooting."

Amos grinned. "I don't c-c-care," he answered stoutly. "I wanted to r-r-run off, anyhow. We'd better be movin' again, hadn't we?"

Jeff nodded and stood up to peer back the way they had come. "Gosh," he frowned. "We've been leaving a trail like a herd o' cattle."

"That's me," Amos replied ruefully. "I'm jest too wide in the beam. We'll have to go separate ways, Jeff. Look, I'll head off to the left, an' if we both come through we'll try an' find each other later."

Jeff was touched by the big youngster's offer, but he shook his head. "No," he said. "We'll stick together, Amos. Make yourself as small as you can, an' come along after me."

Before he had gone another hundred yards he heard the cluck and gurgle of running water close ahead. Pushing through a mat of vines, he found himself on the bank of a tiny brook, a yard or so across. It was not deep. He could see the sand and stones of its bottom quite clearly.

"Here's luck," he told his friend. "We can wade upstream without making any track, and it ought to lead us somewhere near the foot o' the mountain if we follow it far enough."

The water was pleasantly cold to their bare, calloused feet. Overhead, the jungle made a sort of tunnel through which they could move erect most of the time. Jeff stepped carefully to avoid noisy splashing but even so he found the going much faster than it had been before.

The course of the little stream twisted and turned so that they could never see far in front of them. Nevertheless Jeff was satisfied, as they went on, that it was bringing them to higher ground. Several times they had to climb over miniature waterfalls in the brook-bed, and as they hastened upward the growth along the banks changed in character. The trunks of larger trees could be seen, and the great beds of fern had given place to leafy thickets.

The farther they went the smaller the stream became. At last it was a bare trickle among the mossy rocks. Jeff turned off to the left and pushed his way through a clump of bushes with glossy, dark green leaves. His only instinct was to put distance between himself and the beach. He thought they must have come more than a mile now, but there was no telling how straight their direction had been. He shivered as the idea crossed his mind that the rivulet might somehow have led them back toward the spring.

"Hey, wait a bit, Jeff," Amos puffed behind him. "It's goin' to git d-d-dark mighty quick. Sun must ha' set. Hadn't we better be lookin' fer a s-s-safe place to hide?"

Jeff stared around him. It was true. The tropical twilight was coming fast in the jungle. Suddenly a huge tree right ahead of him caught his eye. Its smooth, dark trunk shot upward fifty feet and was lost in a dense mass of leaves. But trailing downward in a loop from the upper branches he saw a rope-like liana as big as his wrist. With an exclamation he leaped forward and put all his weight on the vine. It was supple in his hands but it seemed to be firmly anchored above.

He pulled his belt tighter and looked at his bulky comrade. "Amos," he said soberly. "Get your breath an' spit on your hands. You got to climb now if you never climbed before."

With that he sprang at the liana once more and started up like a monkey, hand over hand. In half a minute he was high among the leaves, swinging his leg over a thick branch close to the trunk.

"Come along," he called softly. "It's strong enough to hold you." And below in the dusk he could catch a glimpse of Amos valiantly starting the ascent. The stout vine creaked complainingly at the strain put upon it, but it held. Foot by foot the heavy lad struggled upward. He had his legs locked around the slippery bark and his arms hauled sturdily. Jeff could feel the big branch shake and sway at each tug. He tried to give Amos encouragement.

"They'll never find us up here," he told him. "It's comfortable, too. There's a wide crotch you can curl up in. Most enough room to lie down and sleep."

A stifled groan was the only answer, but the boy kept on climbing. At last he was close enough for Jeff to reach down and give him a hand, and with a final desperate heave he was hoisted across the limb.

While Amos clung there recovering from his efforts, Jeff looked around to see what security their hiding-place would afford them. It was growing dark so rapidly that he wanted to get his bearings. There were several large branches within reach and any one of them would offer a fairly comfortable perch for the night.

Amos was finally able to draw a long breath. "Show me that c-c-crotch you was tellin' about," he gasped. "I'm ready to go to bed right now!"

Jeff helped him move along the branch till his back was against the tree trunk. Hardly had the boy settled himself when a sound froze them both into motionless silence. From down the hill in the undergrowth came a confused mumble of voices.

CHAPTER XIII

SCARCELY breathing, Jeff crouched on the limb and listened. At first he could not tell how far away the voices might be. Then distinct words came up to him.

"... 'Oo says 'e come this way, any'ow?"

"Naw—it ain't 'im. It's the other two—the fat boy an' that young blackguard, Robbins. 'Ere, bring yer torch closer!"

Through the leaves Jeff could see a moving

flicker of light less than a hundred yards away. It was not approaching in a straight line but zigzagging as if the searchers were casting about for tracks. What if they should come up to the tree and see that tell-tale liana hanging toward the earth!

With the speed of fright the boy scrambled out on the limb and began hauling the heavy vine upward. It was impossible to coil it like a rope, but the fibers were pliant enough so that he could hang long loops across the branch. At last he had pulled up enough of the slack to make the vine almost invisible from the ground. A sleepy bird, roused by the disturbance, squawked protestingly and was quiet again. Jeff did not dare to move. He lay on his stomach with the vine folded under him and wrapped his arms around the limb.

After four or five minutes the torch moved erratically nearer. In the glade below Jeff could make out half a dozen men armed with cutlasses and boarding-pikes. Their leader was easily identified as the bullying bo'sun's mate, Scallon.

"Look there," one of the seamen growled. "Ain't that a track?"

They all squatted around an impression in the dark earth not ten feet from the bottom of the tree.

"Aye," nodded Scallon sagely. " 'Twas made by a 'uman foot, right enough."

Jeff waited in terror, but none of the party so much as glanced upward. They were busy searching the ground beyond.

"Wot if these tracks was made by the natives?" one of the sailors asked the man nearest him.

Scallon overheard him and snorted. "Yer think anybody could live on a speck of an island like this?" he said. "There ain't even a goat 'ere. Nothin' but snakes. An' speakin' o' snakes, I wish I'd wore my sea-boots!"

In another moment the man-hunters had straggled off into the woods. Jeff could hear them thrashing through the underbrush some distance away. He sighed and relaxed a little. For the moment at least they were to be given a respite.

"Hey, Jeff," Amos whispered. "You reckon it's true what they said—about nobody bein' able to live here?"

Jeff set his jaw grimly. "Well," he answered, "looks like we might find out—if they don't catch us first."

He shifted his position a little to get the cramps out of his legs and lay listening for what seemed at least an hour. A long way off he could hear other search parties shouting and swearing as they blundered through the jungle. Half the men from the *Albatross* must be scouring the island tonight, he thought.

At length he caught the sound of Scallon's gang returning. Their voices were gruff with weariness. One of the men must have stumbled over a root for Jeff heard a crash in the brush, followed by a string of profanity. When the smoky flicker of the torch was almost directly under his perch, somebody made a remark that gave the boy a moment of terror.

"I wouldn't wonder if they was up one o' these

trees," grumbled the voice.

" 'Oo's goin' to climb a tree like that 'un?" Scallon snapped in reply. "Six foot through if it's an inch, an' the bark as smooth as yer 'and! I tell yer they're 'id in them mangrove swamps by the shore, an' let 'em rot there, says I."

Tired and disgruntled, the posse trailed off toward the boats. A few minutes later the report of a signal gun echoed over the lagoon. The frigate was calling the hands back aboard. For the rest of the night it appeared that the boys would be safe from discovery.

Jeff rearranged the loops of the liana so that there would be no danger of their sliding off the limb. Then he pulled himself up to a higher bough and found a place where he could sit with his back against a small branch for support. As an extra precaution he took off his belt and buckled his body to the limb behind him. It was tight and uncomfortable, but at least he could not fall off if he went to sleep.

"You going to be all right, Amos?" he whispered down to his friend.

"Sure," the other boy answered drowsily. "I've slep' on softer feather-beds, but it'll do, I reckon. I had a length o' cord in my breeches. Got myself tied on here."

Jeff squirmed himself into the least uncomfortable position he could find, and shut his eyes. Sleep came quickly, for the strain of the escape, added to a long day's labor, had taken a lot out of him. He slumbered heavily for an hour or two, then woke up cold and cramped. Shifting his seat and swinging his arms to start up the circulation, he soon dozed off again. But such sleep as he got from then until daylight was troubled and fitful.

The rustle of the dawn wind and the cries of awakened birds announced the coming of day. Jeff stretched his numb limbs painfully and looked down at Amos. The big youngster groaned and rubbed his eyes, looking around him stupidly.

Jeff laughed. "Bet you don't know where you are," he told him.

The start Amos gave when he got a glimpse

of the ground so far below nearly threw him out of the tree. Fortunately the cord knotted under his arms kept him from falling. He stared up at his friend with a feeble grin. "What we got for breakfast?" he yawned.

Jeff had been feeling the pangs of hunger himself but he tried to speak cheerfully. " 'Twon't hurt you a mite to go without a meal," he said. "Maybe if you lose a few pounds you'll climb better. Right now we're not moving out o' this tree. I reckon it's the safest place on the island."

He unstrapped his belt from the branch and chafed his arms and body to get rid of the numbness. Then he began a careful reconnaissance of their tree-top hideaway. Seen in daylight it had a very different look. The tree itself was unlike any tree Jeff had ever seen in his native New England. Its small, glossy leaves grew so thickly that they almost completely screened the upper branches from the ground, and above him the foliage made a huge green bower, interlaced with boughs. Its height was something he could only guess, but he thought it must be at least a hundred feet.

"Say!" he exclaimed. "I'm going up to the top, Amos. I believe I might get a sight o' the lagoon if I get up high enough."

There were so many limbs that the climb was almost as easy as going up stairs. In a minute or two he found himself far up in the crotch of a slim branch that swayed to the steady rush of the trade wind. The leaves were still thick about him, but by pushing them apart he got a glimpse of sun and sea to the eastward. He worked his way around till he faced north and tried again. There lay the blue lagoon with its outer fringe of surf, and right in the middle, framed by rustling foliage, was the *Albatross,* looking like a picture ship.

She was so near that it seemed as if he could have tossed a stone aboard her. Every rope and spar was clearly outlined in the early morning light. On deck he could see tiny dots of blue that were seamen going about their tasks. The boats, he saw, had all been hove in and lashed in their chocks. He counted them to make sure—long-boat, cutter, gig and jolly-boat—every one was in its proper place. Over the water the breeze brought him a faint sound of singing. The men in the bows were raising a chantey as they walked the capstan 'round.

"Amos!" he called down in his excitement. "She's weighing anchor! An' I can see men on the tops'l yards—making sail, by thunder!"

"Well, what's the trouble?" the other boy asked reasonably. "You don't wish you was ab-b-board her, do you?"

"Why, you lunkhead—it means they've given up looking for us. They're going away. We're free men, Amos!"

But as he watched the frigate slowly gather way and tack out through the pass, he began to wonder. There was something sobering about the idea of being marooned on a desert island. He waited till the *Albatross* was past the reef and the breeze had filled her sails on the long reach to the westward. Then he clambered down.

"Gone, is she?" asked Amos.

Jeff nodded.

"Ye know—I b-b-been thinkin'," the boy stammered. "What if they was tryin' to fool us? S'pose they sailed off in plain sight an' left a gang hid down by the spring to grab us when we showed ourselves."

"Gee, you might be right," Jeff frowned. "An' the spring is just where they'd look for us to come, too. Still, we can't stay here an' starve to death, Amos. I'll go down alone an' do some scouting 'round."

He silenced Amos' objections to this plan by explaining that one could move faster and more quietly than two. "You pull the vine up soon as I'm on the ground, an' keep out o' sight," he told his friend. "If I'm not back in an hour you'll know there's something wrong. But no fear—I'll be back."

He let down the coils of the liana and slid quickly to the earth. After what he had seen in the torchlight the night before, he was careful to step on hard ground, where he left no footprints. In a moment he had slipped silently into the green edge of the jungle.

He stopped to drink at the little brook, but instead of following its bed as before, he crept and wriggled downhill through the rank growth of plants and bushes. Bearing to the left, it was not long before he heard the tinkling splash of falling water, and knew he must be approaching the fountain. From that point on, he crawled on his belly like a snake, pausing every few yards to watch and listen.

At last he was right at the edge of the glade that surrounded the pool. Lying in the ferns he could look between their stems and see all that went on in the open space before him. The scene was reassuring enough. A number of small, bright birds were drinking and preening their feathers on the margin of the spring. As he looked, a pair of green parrots flew down from a palm close by and added their raucous voices to the chirping chorus. If there had been any body of men in the neighborhood it seemed to him that the birds would hardly be so unconcerned.

After watching them awhile he crept down the path a little way, darted across it, and began to scout the jungle on the other side of the pool. Everything was natural and peaceful among the green fronds. He had almost decided there was no ground for Amos' suspicions, when a rustling noise in the undergrowth made him crouch in cold fear.

Something was moving, off there to his right —crawling slowly nearer. He could hear it breathing, panting. Then the movement stopped and he caught the sound of a low, stifled groan.

Jeff got a grip on his nerves and waited. After a moment of silence the groaning came again and this time there were words in it—slurred and hoarse, but recognizable as human speech. The boy got to his feet and moved forward, his caution forgotten as he peered through the leafy thicket. At first he could see nothing. Then he caught a glimpse of tattered blue cloth in the grass, and made out the figure of a man, lying face down.

It was Jonas Beale. In an instant Jeff was

kneeling beside him, horrified at the sight of the dark, bleeding wound in his back. The poor fellow's eyes were closed and his hands clutched convulsively at the soft, black earth.

Jeff lifted him under the arms and half carried, half dragged him out to the edge of the spring. Holding his head on his knee he began scooping up water and sprinkling the pale, dirt-stained face. In a moment Jonas gasped feebly and opened his eyes. They were hazy with pain and they stared past Jeff without recognition. The drawn lips tried to form words, but the only sound that came from them was an unintelligible croaking.

The boy filled both hands with water and let it run down into the wounded man's mouth. He gulped at the cooling drink as if he could never get enough, then choked with a wrenching spasm and hung limp across Jeff's knees.

"Jonas," the lad pleaded, "don't you know me? It's Jeff—Jeff Robbins, from Shinnequid. You're safe now, with Amos an' me. We'll take care o' you, Jonas."

But it was no use. The seaman drew a few short, gasping breaths, then a kind of shiver went through his big frame and he lay very still. Jeff sat there stupefied for half a minute before he realized that his shipmate was dead. Then, in a panic, he laid his ear over the man's heart. It had stopped beating. Slowly he placed the body on the ground and stood up on shaky legs. A shadow seemed to have come over the dazzling brilliance of the tropic morning.

Jeff wanted only to get away from that place. Careless of a possible ambush he walked straight down the path to the beach and stood there staring out across the empty lagoon. In the sand at his feet were the deep grooves made by the beached boats, the maze of the tracks left by the watering party. That was all. No ship. No voices. A white-winged gull wheeled over the lagoon and screamed once, mournfully. In its call the boy felt all the vast loneliness of sea and sky.

CHAPTER XIV

How much time Jeff spent there on the
beach he did not know. He was recalled to
the immediate realities by the sight of a big sea-
turtle crawling laboriously up out of the tide.
The boy had been standing so still that the turtle
paid no attention to him whatever. It heaved its
slow way up the sand, scooped a shallow hole
with its flippers, drew its head into its shell and
settled down as if to sleep.

Jeff turned and started back up the path. He must go and tell Amos what had happened. But before he had walked half the distance to the big tree he heard a commotion in the thicket and saw the bulky shoulders of his friend pushing through a tangle of leaves.

Amos caught sight of him at the same moment. "Where you been?" he asked with a grin of relief. "I waited more'n an hour an' got so hungry I jest had to c-c-climb down. Any Britishers around?"

Jeff shook his head. "No, they've gone," he said. "But I found poor Jonas Beale. Come on with me."

As they went toward the spring he told the whole story. Amos was shocked and upset. "Shot in the back!" he muttered. "The dirty devils! Gosh, Jeff—suppose we'd gone with him when he wanted us to. They'd have g-g-got us sure!"

They carried the dead seaman down the path and laid him on the sand. "We can dig a grave up here above the tide-line," Jeff said. "But before we bury him we ought to look through his pockets. There might be something he'd want us to send home—if we ever get away from here."

" 'Course we'll get away," Amos answered stoutly. "Shouldn't wonder if we was picked up in a week."

Jeff was far less certain, but he said nothing. In Jonas Beale's belt was a heavy seaman's dirk —something neither of the boys had possessed. They took it, together with a pouch containing flint and steel which they found in his pocket. There was nothing else except a shilling or two in change and half a plug of tobacco. These they buried with him. They dug the grave with the staves from a broken water cask, and placed one of them at the head of the mound for a marker.

"Hey—look at that!" Amos exclaimed, as they finished their gloomy task. He pointed down the beach at the turtle, now lumbering sedately toward the water. "Come on, Jeff— mebbe we can c-c-catch him. He'd sure make a mess o' soup!"

Together they made a rush for the big beast and succeeded in heading it off just as it reached the wet line left by the last wave.

"Quick—flip him over!" panted Amos. They seized the side of the huge shell between the flippers and heaved on the two-hundred-pound mass till it toppled over with a thud.

Immediately the turtle pulled its head and legs in for protection. Amos lifted the dirk triumphantly and stabbed downward at the smooth under-side of the shell, but the point of the knife skidded off the horny surface as if it had been an iron plate. The boy looked up at Jeff with an expression of such baffled amazement on his round face that his friend burst into laughter.

"All right," said Jeff, still chuckling. "You've got him. Now what are you going to do with him?"

"Shucks!" Amos answered sheepishly. "He's tougher'n a brick wall—top an' bottom. How'd I know it would take an ax to open him? We ain't got an ax, have we, Jeff?"

Jeff shook his head. "There's a lot o' things we could use if we had 'em, and an ax is one. The way it looks to me, we might as well let him go."

They argued the matter for a few minutes and finally tipped the clumsy brute back onto its belly. The turtle poked its nose out cautiously. When it found that the boys had no further hostile intentions it scrambled into the water with comic haste.

"There goes our turtle soup," Amos mourned as he watched their captive disappear. "Now what are we goin' to eat?"

Jeff was poking with a stick in the dry sand farther up the beach. "Wait a bit," he said. "I reckon maybe it wasn't a 'him' after all. Look at this!" And in triumph he held up a leathery brown globe nearly the size of a hen's egg.

"There's more of 'em in the hole!" he exclaimed. "Eighteen or twenty—and all fresh-laid. I saw her when she came up here."

Amos examined the turtle's eggs with some doubt. "Are they fit to eat?" he asked. "What do you do—cook 'em?"

"We'll try it and find out," Jeff answered practically. He gathered some sticks and dry leaves for tinder and started a fire with the flint and steel. There was no vessel in which to boil water, but as soon as a bed of embers had collected he placed four or five of the eggs in the middle of it and covered them with hot ashes.

"Now, while they're roasting," he told his companion, "we'd better see what else we can find to eat."

Taking different directions, they skirted the more open growth along the base of the mountain. Jeff picked up two or three wind-fallen coconuts in their fibrous brown husks. He also saw what he thought must be banana trees, but the clusters of fruit were too small and green to tempt him.

When Amos rejoined him at the fire a few minutes later, the big fellow was carrying a miscellaneous armful of discoveries.

"No tellin' what these here things are," he grinned, "or whether any of 'em are g-g-good to eat. I jest brung along anything that looked like food!"

"Good lad!" Jeff replied, looking over the assortment. "Those rusty green ones are mangoes

Young Hammersley gave me one to eat, that time we stopped at Jamaica. An' I'd say that thing that looks like a muskmelon might be a papaya. Nate Winslow told me they were real good eating. But let's try the turtle's eggs first. They surely must be done by now."

That was as strange a breakfast as a pair of boys from Maine ever enjoyed. For enjoy it they did. Sitting on the sand in the shade of a rustling palm they first devoured two roast eggs apiece—not bad, they decided, but somewhat flat-tasting without salt. Then they sliced the husk off a coconut, punched out its "eyes" and drank the sweet milk. The mangoes came next. And they topped off the feast with the firm, yellow flesh of the melon-like papaya.

Amos rubbed his paunch contentedly. "No tellin' how such vittles'll set on a New England stomach," he said. "But I got to admit I ain't f-f-felt better fed since I left Shinnequid."

.   .   .   .

Such was the beginning of their life on the island. They settled down to a routine that was peaceful enough, and every day was much like those that went before and came after. The sun blazed on the sand, the wind blew ceaselessly, the birds fluttered and screamed around the fountain. Occasionally the monotony of the weather was broken by a sudden tropical storm, brief but terrible in its violence.

The first of these cloudbursts caught the boys unprepared and they huddled for half a day in the edge of the thick jungle near the beach, while the tall palms whipped back and forth in the blast and the rain roared over in solid sheets. As the storm blew itself out and they crept forth, dripping and bedraggled, into a world of wet, misty sunshine, they saw a sight that neither of them would ever forget.

Off to the northward, across two or three miles of sea, a funnel-shaped black cloud was whirling, its tip reaching down till it nearly met the racing waves. Then the gray water seemed to leap upward, gathering itself in a solid column that merged with the cloud. And the whole spinning mass—water and vapor mingled in the shape of an elm-tree a thousand feet high—marched west-ward over the sea at terrific speed.

Even as the boys watched, speechless, the waterspout broke. Its column seemed to totter and spray outward. An incredible weight of water crashed back into the sea. They heard the sound of it, many seconds later, in a long, moan-ing roar, more terrible than thunder. And after they had left the beach and climbed to the spring, a single mighty wave rolled in, towering over the mangroves and smashing into the jun-gle a full twenty feet above the tide-line.

After that experience Jeff allowed Amos no rest until they discovered a place of shelter. They had already done some exploring along the lower slopes of the mountain. Beyond the line of trees, the rocks soared upward, naked, black and precipitous. But in one place, far around on the northwest shoulder, they found a narrow cave with a stone shelf overhanging its mouth. To reach it, Jeff had to scale an almost vertical cliff a dozen feet high. Once he entered the cave, however, he knew that they could keep dry there in any weather. A deep, irregular passage ran back into the mountain farther than he could see. There was dust on the floor of the cavern that might have been undisturbed for centuries.

That afternoon they built a ladder, tying cross-pieces on a pair of driftwood poles with ropes twisted from palm-leaf fiber. It made the climb easy, even for Amos, and they stocked the cave with coconuts so that they would have food and drink whenever they were driven to take shelter there.

Other journeys of exploration soon showed them that their domain was even more limited than they had supposed. On its eastern and western sides the mountain ran down steeply into deep water, and there was no way to reach the southern part of the island on foot. For a while Jeff considered swimming around one of the cliffs to find out what might lie to the south. But when Amos pointed out the triangular fin of a big gray shark, cruising lazily offshore, he was quite willing to give up the idea.

After that they talked over the possibilities of

being picked up by a passing vessel. There was not enough dry wood to keep a beacon fire burning at night, and they had no way of signaling in daylight. The island seemed to be out of the usual track of ships. Three long weeks went by before they so much as sighted a sail, and then it was a tiny speck far to the northward, that vanished over the horizon in an hour.

Their most likely chance of rescue would be the arrival of a vessel in need of water. But if she turned out to be under the British flag they could never risk showing themselves. Jeff's heart sank sometimes when he thought of the years that might pass before an American ship or even one under French or Spanish registry happened to visit that lost speck on the chart.

At night, lying awake under the stars, he argued with himself. Had he been a silly fool to run away from the *Albatross?* For his own part he would have done the same thing over again. But he knew Amos had taken the step only because of his urging. The fact that his friend never complained made his conscience no easier.

Somehow, he vowed to himself, he must manage an escape for both of them.

Aside from the monotony of their daily routine, life on the island was pleasant enough. Jeff invented ways to make their days more interesting and Amos followed his lead with unflagging enthusiasm. They improved the path from the spring to the beach and cut other trails to make their journeys through the jungle easier. For a while they went cautiously, afraid of encountering the snakes Scallon had mentioned. But as no snakes ever showed themselves they moved about with more confidence. They soon located the best places to gather the fruit and coconuts that made up most of their diet. And they experimented with other foods—shell-fish and the tender hearts of young palm tops.

It was Jeff who thought of carrying sea-water in coconut shells to fill shallow depressions in the rocks. The burning sun quickly evaporated the water and when the hollows had been refilled repeatedly for several days, a crust of white began to collect. After that the boys had salt for their food.

The thing they missed most, following months of living on a man-o'-war, was meat. Bananas, mangoes and papayas made an abrupt change after the eternal salt pork of their ship-board diet. Amos searched the beach for hours at a time without discovering any more turtle's eggs. It appeared that their first find had been a lucky one. However, a few weeks after they were marooned, Jeff came across another turtle on the sand and succeeded in killing it. This one was less than two feet long and the hide between the breastplate and upper shell was soft enough to cut through with the dirk. They roasted some of the flesh that night and found it tender and palatable. After that they dined on fresh turtle meat as often as they could make a catch.

At first they made some plans to build a hut. There were enough fallen trees and pieces of driftwood to make a framework, and it would have been easy to thatch the walls and roof with palm fronds. But for several reasons Jeff decided against the idea.

"Suppose the *Albatross* comes back to look for us," he argued. "Or just as bad—some other British frigate or ship. We don't want 'em to find anything like a house. Besides, soon as one o' those hurricanes comes along it'll be blown to kingdom come. We've got the cave for a hideout an' for stormy weather, so we might as well sleep out on fair nights."

For the chill that came after sundown they wove palm-leaf mats, half a dozen feet square, and with these wrapped around them they slept on the sand with a fair degree of comfort.

There were so many other things to occupy their time that it was a full month before they revisited the cave. Then one day when Jeff was feeling restless, he proposed that they really explore its deeper recesses.

"We might as well know what's there," he told Amos. "Some day, if we were being chased, it wouldn't hurt to have a secret hole to duck into."

"How we goin' to find our way without a light?" the other boy replied. "It's darker'n pitch when ye git back aways."

"That's what I've been thinking about. We've got to make torches that'll burn awhile."

They tried twisting dry grass into tight bundles, but though these gave a bright flare they lasted only half a minute. Stalks of various weeds proved too green to do more than smoke and smolder. Finally, after half a day of experimenting, they found a shrub with oily sap which burned steadily and gave a clear, yellow flame.

Gathering a supply of the wood and some dry leaves for tinder, they climbed the ladder to the cave-mouth.

The pile of coconuts they had left inside was undisturbed. Enough daylight came in at the entrance to make the irregular walls of the cavern visible for perhaps thirty feet, but beyond that point the space narrowed and made a bend, so that the boys peered into absolute darkness. They stopped there and lighted a torch. With Jeff holding it above his head and Amos carrying an armful of spare sticks, they advanced warily into the rocky passage.

CHAPTER XV

COMING as they had from the hot sun, the air in the cave felt chilly. Jeff shivered once or twice as he moved forward. The floor of the passage was a rough ledge, sloping to one side, and its walls were of natural rock formation, all crannies and hollows and jutting shoulders of stone.

Before they had gone twenty feet beyond the bend, a rustling sound overhead stopped them in their tracks. Black shadows flittered through the torchlight, and Jeff felt a rush of wings close to his cheek.

"Bats!" he said between chattering teeth. "Hanging to the roof. The smoke an' the light roused 'em out."

They recovered their courage and went forward, a step at a time. Ahead of them the cavern appeared to come to a dead end. Then, as they drew closer, they saw a narrow opening to the left, hardly wide enough for a man's body to pass through. But it was the rock wall in front of them that held their attention. Cut crudely into the flat surface was a symbol made by human hands.

What they saw was a rough numeral VI surrounded by a square, each side of which measured about a foot. At the left of the square a broad arrow had been carved, pointing in the direction of the little passage.

"Somebody cut that in the rock!" Jeff exclaimed. His voice dropped to a whisper, as if he might be overheard.

"Yeah," Amos answered. "But who c-c-could

it ha' been?"

Jeff held the light closer. "It's old. Might have been 'most anybody that stopped at the island in the last two hundred years. What I want to know is where it points—an' why!"

They squeezed through the opening in the left wall and found themselves suddenly in a much larger cavern, many yards in width and so high that the roof was lost in the dark.

"Gosh!" they murmured, both at once, and as if the word had been a signal the torch flickered and went out.

In absolute darkness Jeff fumbled for the tinder and the flint and steel. It seemed like hours before his efforts brought forth a spark and a trembling pin-point of flame. At last they managed to light another of their greasewood torches and stood up to look around in wonder.

This inner cave, like the passage through which they had entered, bore no evidence of the work of men. It was a strange natural formation in the lava rock. The irregular roundness of its sides and floor suggested that a gigantic bubble of gas or steam had been imprisoned there until the molten stone had cooled. The fissure into the outer cave must have been caused by an earthquake at some later time.

They went forward, stepping over loose rubble and staring upward into shadowy depths above them. "It's as big as—as a church!" Jeff said in awe, and his voice rang through the space with a metallic echo. When they had made the circuit of the cave and returned to their starting point, the two boys looked at each other in puzzlement.

Jeff scratched his head with his free hand. "The fellow that cut those marks outside meant something by it," he said. "Maybe he'd found something here—or hid something. Maybe he wanted to come back to it a long time after. You an' I've got to figure out what he meant, Amos."

The other lad nodded excitedly. "You reckon that number six stands f-f-for feet?" he asked.

"Might be. Or paces, perhaps. It's most likely something to do with a measurement."

"Where would it start from? Right here by the entrance?"

"Seems probable. Anyhow, we can't do more than try."

Jeff held the torch down close to the threshold of the opening. "Look there!" he cried. "We walked right over it when we came in!"

Half covered with dust and bits of crumbled stone there was a straight line, about a yard long, carved in the floor.

"That's your starting-point!" Jeff told his friend. "Now let's see where we get if we go six feet out from here."

They measured the distance as exactly as they could without a foot rule and searched the floor of the cave for a yard around the spot. There was nothing there that could possibly be a hiding-place for any object bigger than a pin.

"Must be paces," said Amos. "Here, I'll start off an' you tell me if I keep in a straight line."

He took six generous strides, starting with his heel on the chiseled line. When he stopped Jeff brought the light and joined him in an examination of the ground. Two or three larger stones were moved without disclosing anything of interest. A few feet away they found a cranny in the floor, into which Amos immediately thrust his hand. It was several inches wide and wrist-deep, and at first they thought they had discovered the secret. But when both boys had had a turn at exploring the crevice with searching fingers they were forced to admit it was a false clue.

"Here," said Jeff, trying not to show his disappointment, "we'd better get a fresh torch lighted before this one goes out. I've used up all the tinder."

When the new stick was burning they stood there in thoughtful silence, trying to work the problem out. At the end of a long minute, Amos' wrinkled brows cleared. "I been thinkin'," he said. "That number six is in a box, like—with f-f-four sides to it. How 'bout tryin' six paces, four times? That's twenty-four, ain't it?"

Jeff nodded. "There must be a reason for the number to be in a box. Maybe you've hit on it, Amos. Only it could be feet. Now, let's see— twenty-four feet would be eight yards. Take two more paces from here an' that's what we'll have."

Eagerly they bent over the rocky floor, peering into every crack, turning over pebbles, stamping with their feet and listening for a hollow sound. It was no use.

Amos shook his head. "I figgered it must be in paces," he said, "an' it sure ain't feet. Here— I'm goin' to start f-f-fresh off the mark."

Stepping off twenty-four yards brought him almost to the center of the cavern. Jeff, watching at the line to make certain he moved straight, hastened after him as soon as he stopped. Automatically, to himself, he had been repeating the multiplication table—"six times four are twenty-four—six times five are thirty—six times six—" and at those words something clicked in his mind.

"Amos," he said, "I believe I've got it! You take the torch and hunt here. I want to try something."

Carefully he sighted the line to the cave entrance, then turned and took twelve more paces away from it. At the last stride his bare toe stubbed against a big stone in the semi-darkness, and muttering his exasperation, he sat down on the boulder to rub the bruise.

As he leaned forward he felt his seat rock gently under him. It was a big, smooth stone shaped like a slightly flattened egg, a yard long and nearly two feet through. At a guess it would weigh at least three hundred pounds. Forgetting his toe for the moment, he jumped up and pushed on the rock with his hand. Again he felt it move as if it had slipped a little on its base.

"Amos," he called, trying to keep the excitement out of his voice. "You finding anything there?"

"Nothin' yet," his friend sighed.

"Well, come here a minute."

Amos laid down his remaining sticks of greasewood to mark the spot and brought the light to Jeff's side. "What's this got to do with six times four?" he asked. "You're way out on yer calculation!"

"Just wait and see. I've got a hunch—here, we'll both lift together under this end."

Amos stuck the torch in a cleft of rock and they heaved in unison. The boulder moved a few inches.

"Again!" panted Jeff. "That's it! Now—once more for luck!"

The huge stone tilted for an instant on its rounded side, then rolled over with a crunch and a rumble that reverberated through the cave. Where it had previously rested, the boys saw the mouth of a hole yawning darkly.

Jeff snatched up the torch and held it close with hands that trembled. The flickering light was reflected by hinges of hammered brass. Down there in the hole, a foot below the cave floor, a dark old wooden chest lay buried!

"What in t-t-tarnation—" gasped Amos, falling on his knees and tugging at the handle of the box. "Gosh—she's heavy, Jeff! It'll take the two of us to git her out!"

Placing the torch in the cleft again, Jeff hastened to join his companion. He was kneeling beside the hole and had just got his fingers through the metal handle of the chest when he heard a little clattering sound behind him. Then the cavern was plunged into pitch-darkness. The blazing stick had tumbled from its cranny and gone out.

There was a disgusted snort from Jeff and then silence.

"What are we g-g-goin' to do now?" gurgled Amos. He was having a hard time holding back a chuckle.

"We're going to haul this chest out, light or no light," Jeff answered firmly. "Then we'll see about finding our way back."

The box, as Amos had discovered, was amazingly heavy for its size. It was all the boys could do to hoist it up to the floor of the cavern.

"Now," said Jeff, "before we move we'd better get our bearings straight. Near as I can figure, the cave wall is right back o' me a little way—an' the place we came in is over there."

"Over where?" Amos' voice same sepulchrally out of the darkness.

"I'm pointing. Here—feel my hand?"

"That ain't the way I remember. Still, I

reckon you're right about the wall an' we can feel our way along till we find a hole in it. You want to start? I'm ready."

They staggered to their feet with the box between them, and Jeff felt his way back until the upward slope of the floor made him certain the side of the cave was near.

"Let's put it down a minute," he said. "Sure is heavy. Heavy as lead! I want to feel around back here till I reach the wall. You'd better stay where you are an' keep talking, so I can find you again."

Two or three more cautious steps brought his hand into contact with upright stone. He touched it here and there and felt a crack in the rock surface just above his head. Loosened by his fingers a shower of rubble came down and then suddenly the blackness around him seemed full of roaring, fiery sparks.

.   .   .   .

When Jeff struggled back to consciousness he was blinking up into the green fronds of a palm tree that stirred and rustled in the wind. His head felt too big for his body. There was an ache in it—a dull, steady throbbing. Through the pain his mind groped for a hint of what had happened. Then he saw Amos' perturbed face leaning above him and remembered the cave and the darkness.

"What hit me?" he asked weakly. "How'd you get me out?"

"Don't try to do no talkin' now," Amos answered gently. "I'm all-fired glad to see yer eyes open, though. I couldn't tell what happened in the dark, but I reckon 'twas a l-l-loose rock fell on ye. Had sort of a time haulin' ye out o' there, but I found the passageway after a spell. It's been four or five hours—most sunset now. How ye feel?"

Jeff managed half a grin. "Better—now I know I'm alive," he murmured. "Didn't crack my skull bone, did it?"

"Not as near as I can tell. It raised a turrible lump, but I been puttin' cold water on it. Why don't ye try an' git some sleep now? I'll tap a coconut an' give ye the milk by-an'-by."

Jeff's eyes were closed but he was still remembering. "Where's the chest?" he asked.

"Chest? Danged if I hadn't fergot there was such a thing! Why, she lays where we dropped her, I reckon. Right there in the cave."

"I'd give a lot to know what's in it," the injured boy murmured sleepily. "We'll go back there, soon as—soon as—"

But before he finished the sentence a great drowsiness overtook him. He must have slept a solid twelve hours, for dawn was breaking and the parrots had begun to scream in the trees when he woke again. His head still hurt but the throbbing ache was gone. Gingerly he sat up and looked around him. At his side was the faithful Amos, snoring gently. On the ground between them lay a green coconut, husked and ready to be tapped. With a stroke of the dirk Jeff cut the top off and took a long drink of the cool, refreshing juice.

He left his friend still slumbering and went quietly toward the foot of the rock where their home-made ladder stood. Weak as he was, he had an overpowering curiosity about the brass-bound box. But even as he placed a foot on the lowest rung he remembered what the cave was like in the dark, and turned back regretfully. Before any new attempt could be made they must have plenty of torch-sticks and tinder.

He was hunting through the underbrush for greasewood shrubs and had quite a pile of the stuff collected when Amos hailed him in outraged tones.

"Great land o' Goshen!" shouted the boy. "You tryin' to kill yerself? C-c-come here an' lay in the shade till I git breakfast!"

In strict truth Jeff was glad enough to sit down for a while, but he laughed at his companion's fears. "I'll be as good as ever in another day," he told him. "We can't wait that long to look at the chest, though. I've been cutting wood for lights, so we can start in right away."

Amos outdid himself on that breakfast. He had found a nest of good-sized bird's eggs somewhere in the woods, and these he set to cook in one of the empty coconut shells they used for pots and pans. Placed among the hot embers, such a utensil was good for a meal or two before it charred through. Meanwhile the lad hurried off into the jungle and returned with an armful of ripe fruit.

Rested, Jeff found he had a good appetite. As soon as the meal was finished he stood up and faced the rock ledge below the cave. "I'll take the light-wood and the tinder," he announced. "And you cut us one o' those tough vines over yonder. We can use it for a rope to drag the chest out."

When Amos joined him at the top of the ladder he had a dozen feet of flexible liana coiled in his hand. They lighted a torch and went into the cave at once.

This time their expedition moved faster, for they knew the way. Within two minutes they had entered the big, inner cavern and knotted an end of the liana firmly to a handle of the box. With the rope-vine over their shoulders they found it easier to pull the heavy weight along the floor than to carry it. Quickly the chest was lifted through the opening to the outer cave and dragged along to the ledge in front of the en-trance.

The effort had made Jeff's head ache again and he felt a little dizzy. "I'm going to sit here for a minute and rest," he told Amos with a grin. "But I'm sure wild to know what's in it. Go ahead—see if you can open that lock."

CHAPTER XVI

THE CHEST, now that they could look at it in daylight, appeared to be very old. Its thick oak sides were worn and darkened with age, and the heavy brass hinges and corner fittings were crusted with green. In size it was about eighteen inches long and a foot wide, with a depth of perhaps nine inches. A brass bar in front was slotted over a staple and held with an ancient iron padlock, so rusted it looked like a shapeless brown lump.

Amos fingered the lock and shrugged his shoulders. "Only one way to open her," he said. "An' that's to b-b-bust her with a rock!"

He hunted along the ledge till he found a round lava cobble nearly as big as his head. With a crash he brought the stone down on the padlock and it dropped off in two rusty pieces. Breathlessly the boys leaned forward over the box as he heaved up the lid.

At first all they saw was brown canvas, shredded and disintegrating with age. But through its tatters something caught the sunlight with a yellow gleam.

Jeff plunged his hand through the rent in the cloth. Speechless, he held up a broad disc of gold. It fell back from his fingers and clinked dully against a heap of similar coins hidden under the rags.

His voice, when he found it, was hoarse with excitement. "Gold!" he said. "It's full o' Spanish gold, Amos!"

"J-j-jumpin' Jehoshaphat!" whispered the

TUCKED IN A CORNER WAS A TINY
BUCKSKIN BAG

other boy. "An' more'n a hundredweight of it! H-h-how much is that in our money, you reckon, Jeff?"

"I dunno! Hundreds—maybe thousands o' dollars, I guess. If we ever get off this island we're going to be rich, Amos!"

They began taking the gold pieces out and stacking them beside the box. They were all alike, some worn with use, some freshly minted, but every one bearing the likeness of a man and a Spanish inscription that looked like "CARLOS II RE."

Only about half the contents of the chest turned out to be gold pieces. Below was another old sack of big silver coins. And tucked away in a corner was a tiny buckskin bag, brittle with years, in which they found a dozen softly gleaming, iridescent pearls.

There was no writing on the box, no paper or parchment inside, to tell them who had hidden the treasure in the cave. When they had replaced its contents and carried it back into the darkness of the passage, they spent an hour or two talking about this former owner.

"I'd guess he was a Spanish ship-captain," Jeff concluded. "He was coming out from Spain, because if he'd been going the other way he'd have been carrying bullion, from Peru or Panama. Then Morgan or Drake or one o' those old buccaneers got after him an' he put in here to hide. For safekeeping he buried the chest in the cave and cut his mark on the rock, hoping to send somebody after it later—"

"Say," Amos interrupted. "That makes me think—you n-n-never told me how you figgered where to look."

Jeff laughed. " 'Twas lucky I remembered some o' my school arithmetic," he said. "Six times six is the 'square' o' six, see? I thought maybe that's what he meant by putting a square around the number, so I walked off thirty-six paces an' bumped right into it!" He rubbed his bruised bare toe at the memory.

As they discovered, when their first excitement was over, the sudden access of riches made very little difference in their way of living. Spanish gold would buy no food or clothing on an island where there were no people. It added little to their comfort but it did serve to whet their appetites for escape.

Jeff lay awake for hours that night. He had considered every possibility of getting away from the island a hundred times before, but now he went over the facts again and again. The idea of waiting through months and perhaps years for the arrival of a friendly ship went against his grain. And yet—what else could they do? If the luck that had led them to the treasure chest had given them tools instead, they might have had a better chance. An ax, a saw and a hammer would at least have let them make an attempt at building a boat. But with nothing but a seaman's knife the task was plainly impossible.

One thought kept repeating itself in the boy's troubled mind. It was that until now they knew nothing about the other side of the island. There was a remote chance that beyond the mountain, on the southern slope, people might once have lived—might have left tools, or even a completed boat. He knew better than to believe there were any living inhabitants. If that were the case, some canoe or fishing boat would surely have made its appearance in the two months the boys had been marooned.

Still wrestling with the problem, Jeff fell at last into a troubled sleep. He dreamed a good deal that night—fantastic dreams in which he struggled over mountains and through swamps, pursued by queer people. But the last one, still vivid in his memory when he woke, gave him a new idea. It carried him back to a day in Shinnequid Cove when he was a little boy. On the rocky shore he had found a drifting hatch-cover, washed in from some wrecked coasting schooner. He had launched it, mounted a stick amidships for a mast, stretched a bit of old canvas, and sailed his waterlogged raft for nearly half a mile before the tide had stranded him on the beach. The exploit had filled him with pride at the time, even when he got a spanking for it. In his dream, strangely enough, the raft had been made of palm logs, lashed together with rope, and the sail had been a mat woven of palm fronds.

Wide awake, he reached over and shook Amos' shoulder.

"Get up here, lad!" he cried exultantly. "We've a job to do today!"

While they were rustling up a breakfast he unfolded his plan to his friend. "We could build it quicker if we had an ax," he admitted. "But we can burn the trunks off to make 'em the right length. The raft doesn't have to be very big. Six or eight logs ought to be enough to carry me. And I'm only going a couple of miles—just around to the south side of the island. Come on— let's see what we can find in the way of timber!"

Over toward the eastern shoulder of the mountain they came to a place where a summer hurricane had blown down a clump of several good-sized palms. The wood was partially dried but still sound. Putting their backs into it, they dragged the top of one tree a little apart from the rest and built a fire under it. Burning the log in two turned out to be a long process. To gain speed they started several fires at different points along the fifty-foot trunk, and tended them all day.

It was after sunset when the last log had burned cleanly through. They had four straight lengths of palm wood, each nearly a dozen feet long and from ten inches to a foot and a half in thickness. Jeff looked at the row of timbers with satisfaction. "There's a mighty good start on our raft," he said. "Tomorrow we'll fix another tree the same way an' we'll have a plenty."

Two days of rain that followed kept them from carrying out the plan. But Jeff used the time to scour the jungle, searching for the longest and strongest lianas that grew on the island. When the storm cleared, the evening of the second day, he came in drenched and shivering but triumphant. The long, rope-like vine he threw on the pile gave them a total of more than two hundred feet of liana to work with.

They burned another tree trunk into sections the next day and dragged their logs, one by one, down to the nearest beach. Close to the tide-line they ranged the timbers side by side, and slept by them to make sure they did not float away. In the morning the most interesting part of the job began.

Hunting through the fallen timber, Jeff selected three straight young trees and trimmed them into poles, long enough to reach across the raft and stick out a foot or two at either side. These had to be lashed firmly to the logs. They laced the tough vines in and out, over and under, till at last the platform of logs made a rigid unit, strong enough to stand the heaving of ordinary waves.

Luckily, Jeff had had the foresight to pull the logs farther down the sand and do the work while the tide was out. Otherwise they could never have moved the solid weight of timber. When the sea began rising again the raft was finished. Proudly they watched it float free. As they had hoped, the seasoned wood was buoyant enough to ride with its top well above the water.

"Now," said Jeff, rubbing his hands, "we've got to step some sort of a mast an' yard, an' make us a sail. Reckon I'll have to whittle me out a pair of oars, too. Then, by the great hook block, I'll be ready to navigate her clear round the island!"

Two more days of hard work were required to finish those preparations. Amos undertook the weaving of palm leaves into a sail. It was a long, slow, painstaking job, but he stuck at it patiently. When he finally bound off the edges he had a stiff, irregular mat, roughly six feet square.

Jeff meanwhile was bracing an upright pole in the middle of the raft and setting about the fashioning of paddles. In order to get a fairly broad blade he had to whittle down the shaft of each oar from a six-inch log. By the time the second one was finished his right hand was blistered and raw.

At last a bright morning dawned when everything was in readiness for a trial voyage. The raft had been moored to a stake driven above high-water mark, and they waited for the incoming tide to float it. Jeff lashed the yard, carrying the improvised sail, to the masthead. Tough cords of twisted fiber were attached to the lower corners and served as sheet-ropes.

"All right," said Jeff. "Let's shove her off an' see how she behaves." At the next wave they heaved the raft free and he sprang aboard. With one of the oars he pushed out through the low surf into the lagoon.

Of all the craft he had ever tried to handle, this was the clumsiest. It moved so sluggishly through the water that in ten minutes he had paddled less than a hundred yards from shore. The sail jerked and slatted in the breeze but seemed to have no effect on his progress. And when he finally swung the rough bow over to port and got the yard squared to a quartering wind, the raft displayed an incurable tendency to slide off to leeward.

By dint of hard paddling he managed to keep offshore and bring his sluggish vessel around to a landing on the beach near the spring.

"How's she sail?" asked Amos as he helped haul the raft ashore. "Ain't terrible f-f-fast, is she?"

"No," said Jeff gloomily. "She'll do, though,

for what I want of her. Only thing she needs is a keel or a centerboard. Makes too much leeway, the way she is now."

They puzzled over the problem of the keel for most of the day. It was Amos who found a way to solve it. "Look," he exclaimed suddenly. "Them old barrel-staves up there! Couldn't ye d-d-drive 'em through betwixt the logs? Three or four staves might be as good as a centerboard."

They tried it and found it worked. Jeff improved on the plan by tying the tops of the row of staves together between two saplings, so that they were kept from slipping through the crevice.

"I reckon she's as ready as she'll ever be," he told his chum as darkness gathered. "Tomorrow morning I'll make an early start. The breeze'll favor me the first part o' the way, an' I ought to be 'round the point in a couple of hours. Maybe I'll be back before nightfall if I have luck."

He was so confident of the success of his venture that he fell asleep at once and slumbered soundly till daybreak. With the first light he was up and making final preparations. Amos got their breakfast in silence. He seemed to have lost his cheerfulness that morning, but Jeff was too much absorbed to wonder about it.

He was busy gathering provisions for his day's trip. For a food supply he collected a cluster of half-ripe bananas and a couple of green "drinking" coconuts. As an afterthought he filled a coconut shell with spring water and plugged the holes with wooden stoppers.

The moment breakfast was over he was ready to start. It was then that he noticed Amos' long face.

"Hey," he said, "what's come over you, lad?"

Amos shook his head. "I was only wishin' the durn contraption was b-b-big enough to hold two of us," he replied sadly. "Seems like I'll be worryin' about ye all day."

"Shucks!" Jeff laughed. "I won't get half a mile from shore any place. An' I've got oars, haven't I? It's slow rowing, I'll agree, but there's nothing to worry about."

Amos managed a wan grin. "All right," he said. "I know it ain't really dangerous. I'll be up on the side o' the mountain beyond the cave, where I can keep watchin' as long as ye're in sight. But here—ye g-g-got to take this, Jeff."

He held out the flint and steel. Jeff protested that he would have no need for a fire, but his friend was insistent. "Can't never tell," he said. "A light might come in awful handy, when ye're in a s-s-strange part o' the island."

Jeff was in too great a hurry to spend time in argument. He pocketed the implements and a moment later they were shoving the raft out into the little fringe of breakers. The lagoon was blue and sparkling under the early sun. With a high heart Jeff poled forward into deeper water and turned his unwieldy craft westward. As the wind caught the sail he pushed his barrel-stave center-board down through the cleft between the two middle logs and waved a gay farewell to Amos, who stood forlornly on the beach.

CHAPTER XVII

JEFF had a right to be proud of the way his
home-made vessel behaved. There was nothing resembling speed in his progress, but he had
never expected that. Under the steady push of
the northeast trade wind, the raft slogged along
at a mile or two an hour. It took a frequent use
of the steering oar to keep her on her course, but
the centerboard had considerably reduced the
amount of leeway she made.

CLEAR FOR ACTION!

The boy squatted a little aft of the mast and watched the shoreline slowly change pattern. At the end of an hour he was abreast of the western headland, where the mountain dipped steeply into the sea. He wondered if Amos was up there on the shoulder as he had promised. He was too far out to make sure, but he thought there was a tiny white speck there among the trees.

He was steering in a more southerly direction now, as he came around the point. The wind, instead of being dead astern, blew from the port quarter. He would keep it as long as he could, he decided, before starting to row.

Gradually the loom of the mountain cut down the breeze. The sail began to flap languidly and the air felt hot and still. He saw that he was farther out from shore than he had intended. The distance looked like a full three quarters of a mile. Spitting on his calloused palms, he laid the oars in the chocks he had cut, just aft of the middle cross-brace, and began to pull with a will.

A glance at the island encouraged him. He seemed to be making even more rapid progress than when he had had the wind. It was possible now to catch glimpses of the unexplored southern slope beyond the headland, but though he had swung the raft's bow toward shore those fringing palm trees were as far away as ever. At the end of five more minutes of hard rowing a vague uneasiness entered the boy's mind. The raft was moving sidewise, not forward. He was passing the island instead of approaching it.

He stared at the little blue waves that danced by so innocently and felt a sudden chill of fear. His awkward craft was in the grip of a current, hurrying him southwestward at a faster and faster pace!

In panic he seized the oars again and rowed with all his might. The heavy blades surged through the water but he could not gain against the pull of the tide. Still he worked in a sort of blind frenzy until his arms quivered with fatigue. And at last, when he could no longer lift the oars, he fell back helpless on the round palm logs.

For several moments Jeff lay there gasping, staring up into the blue sky. When he raised himself on one elbow and looked again at the land there could be no question. The intervening stretch of lagoon was widening swiftly. Nothing he could do would change the fact that he was being borne out to sea.

An impulse came to him then. He could make more headway swimming against the current than trying to row the heavy raft. In another instant he would have plunged overboard if he had not chanced to see the lazy gray fin of a shark slipping through the waves between him and the shore. With a shiver the boy settled down again on the sturdy timbers.

After a little he fought down the terror that had first seized him and began to think his situation out. At the rate the raft was moving, it would reach the outer reef in another half hour. There was nothing he could do to stop it. If it struck, the logs must surely break up, and that would be the end of his adventure. If it crossed the reef without disaster, the whole empty Caribbean lay before him—league on league of shifting currents and sudden storms—a slow torture of thirst and hunger that might drag on for hopeless weeks.

Those were his prospects, none too bright, he admitted to himself with a twisted attempt at a grin. But for once in his life, no effort he could make would change the course of fate. He might as well sit quiet in the shade of the idle sail and wait for whatever happened.

The tide had been nearing the full when he pushed off that morning. It was ebbing now but it must still be fairly high. As the raft approached the reef he could see that no jagged coral was exposed. But there were swirling eddies of foam where the tide and current met the low breakers. He clutched the mast and waited.

The heavy craft was hurrying now, like a horse going at a jump. An incoming wave tossed the forward end high and swung the logs in a dizzy spin. There was a jarring check, then another wave swept the raft upward and out. To Jeff's astonishment he was over the reef, and though the centerboard was smashed to bits, the tough liana bindings still held firm beneath him.

He crawled aft to make sure none of his supplies had been washed overboard. The sight of the coconuts made him thirsty but he decided to wait. It was only common sense to ration out his slim stock of provisions and make them last as long as possible. There was still a remote chance that when the tide turned the current might set back toward the island, but he was not counting on any such miracle.

His will to live was as strong as ever. He meant to fight for all the time that was left him and to do that he knew he must conserve his energy. He lay down again in the shadow of the sail and looked back at the receding land.

Even at that distance he could see that no settlement had ever been made on the southern shore. The mountain rose out of the water in cliffs that were nearly as unscalable as those on its flanks. There was no sign of a beach. Behind the few straggling trees at the edge of the lagoon a wall of dark rock went up in a sheer precipice. So his voyage of exploration was vain in any case. He would have had to return to Amos empty-handed.

At the thought of the other boy waiting patiently back there on the northwest cliff he got a lumpy feeling in his throat. Amos deserved something better than the awful loneliness he would know as the days passed.

As the current swept him out from the lee of the island, he could feel the breeze coming again. It stirred the braided palm leaves of the mat and drew the sheet-ropes taut. Jeff got up with the intention of furling the sail and lashing it to the yard. He had slacked off one sheet before he changed his mind. After all, there was nothing to be gained by slowing the raft's progress. If he let wind and current carry him far enough there must be land ahead—the coast of South America—or another island, perhaps.

Thoughtfully he sat down again. There were many uncertainties in the idea, but it held a ray of hope. The current, for instance—how could he tell how far it ran in one direction? The wind, in this latitude, was a fairly fixed quantity. As long as the current helped he could count on being pushed along at a steady twenty or thirty miles every twenty-four hours. If a cross-current took him, or a storm came over—but there was no use even thinking of that. He curled up at the foot of the mast and tried to sleep.

.   .   .   .

When the boy roused himself once more it was nearly sunset. The raft had swung about and was drifting broadside to the breeze, the sail twisting and straining against the sheet-ropes. Jeff took an oar and sculled the stern around till she was before the wind. Then he sat steering for a while. Under him the long swell heaved the logs and ground them together. The lianas creaked as if they would break but he could see that they were still in place. Almost dead ahead the fiery ball of the sun dropped downward into the sea, and the colors faded swiftly around him. He picked up his coconut-shell canteen, pulled the plug with care and took a sparing drink. The bananas, he saw, had ripened fast during the day. If he tried to keep them too long they would spoil, so he decided to eat one. When it was finished he felt hungrier and thirstier than before.

That night, as he steered, he found a sort of peace. What lay ahead was out of his hands. There was nothing to plan for, nothing to fear. Not even the prospect of death could terrify him during those quiet hours under the slowly moving stars.

Calmly he thought back across his seventeen years. His life, that had so often seemed to him drab and dull, was full of pictures that he wanted to keep by him. The lighthouse was the central point in all his earlier memories. He could barely recall his mother's face, for she had died when he was five. After that he had often gone out in the dory with his father to trim the lamp or polish the glass in the stone tower on Tombstone Reef.

Then there had been school, in the little white building at the head of the cove. And summers and Saturdays there were the boats and the lobster-pots. He had turned sailor as naturally as a duck learns to swim.

He remembered the first time he had ever seen Patience Deering, riding in the chaise with the squire along the back road. They were important folks—the Deerings. Too good for a longshore boy like him, he had figured. For a long time he had never dared speak to Patience, bashful as he was. Then there had been a party at a neighbor's house and with a kind of desperate boldness he had asked her to be his partner in a square dance. After that he saw her more often—even went to her house for dinner once or twice. He remembered the cookies and the knitted vest she had brought to the dock, that day the *Abigail* sailed. It was a sweet thing to do, and a brave thing. All those men couldn't scare her. And he had never even worn the vest. It was in the bottom of his sea-bag, aboard the frigate—if they hadn't already divided up his belongings.

Jeff wondered if Patience would miss him, when the war was over and he never came back.

He must have dozed a little before dawn, for he was dreaming when a slosh of salt water in his face woke him. The breeze had freshened and choppy waves were breaking over the raft. He got up stiffly and held onto the mast while he looked around the horizon. The sun was an hour old. Off to the left of it, a little north of east, he could see the dim, blue cone of the island, twenty miles astern. By noon it would be out of sight.

He made sure his provisions had not washed away, and to keep them safe he used his ragged shirt for a sack and tied them up to the cross-trees. Then he trimmed the sail and lay down again. It was a long, difficult day. He tried to keep his mind off the dryness in his throat by repeating all the poetry he had ever had to learn in school. After that he went on to hymns and sea-chanteys. And finally he amused himself by composing long letters in his mind—letters to his father and to Patience—giving a full account of his adventures.

In spite of the breeze the sun burned his already brown body, and he shifted his position as the raft swung, to keep in the shade of the matting. Twice he allowed himself the luxury of a little water, and toward evening he ate another banana.

By the third day Jeff knew the hardship was beginning to tell on him. His head felt light, and when he got on his feet he had a slight spell of dizziness. It was a real effort to keep to his schedule of rations, for there was a fierce gnawing in his stomach that would not be quieted.

That night he opened one of the coconuts and drank its contents, a slow sip at a time. That made him feel better for a while. He must have drowsed a good deal during the next forty-eight hours, for he remembered very little that happened. But some time during his fifth night at sea, the wind shifted. He woke from a heavy sleep with a strange feeling of alertness. Instead of the constant light breeze, the air was coming in uncertain puffs, and by the stars he knew it was from the south. Did that mean a storm was blowing up?

Through the darkness he sat watching, waiting. No clouds came to obscure the sky but he was uneasy, nevertheless. With daylight the wind steadied but it still blew from a southerly quarter. The sea was a different color—a grayer blue —and a thin haze was over the sun.

The raft pitched roughly in the cross-chop and some of the vine ropes were fraying where the logs chafed them. As the haze spread ominously up across the sky, the last tiny shred of hope to which Jeff had clung deserted him. He knew now that the raft could never bring him to land. Late in the afternoon, with a feeling that what he did could make no difference, he ate the last half-rotten banana and drank what was left of the water. When it was gone, he clenched his jaws to stop their trembling, and prayed briefly for courage to meet what was coming like a man and a seaman.

The whole southern half of the sky was shrouded in black now, and the air had a heavy feel. When the dim sun was near the horizon it vanished into a bank of copper-colored cloud. What it was that made Jeff look eastward at that moment he never knew, but there in the swiftly deepening dusk he saw topsails!

It was a schooner, and she was a scant two miles off, across the tossing water. In a delirium of joy the boy waved his arms and shouted hoarsely. Then he saw that the vessel was headed north, before the wind. She would come no nearer on that course. And no lookout would notice such a tiny thing as his raft in the dusk that was already on the sea.

A light—if only he had a light! In a flash of inspiration he remembered the flint and steel. Amos had made him take the pouch and it had lain forgotten in his pocket ever since. With fumbling haste he tugged it out. There was only one thing he could burn—the woven mat he used for a sail. And he had no tinder. Crouching by the mast and sheltering his hands from the wind, he struck the flint against the pan. A spark jumped true, flared for a second in the dry edge of a palm frond, and went out. He tried it again and again, his fingers shaking with despair. Once more the spark flew. And this time the flame lived, flickered higher, roared into a blaze. A puff of wind lifted red crackling tongues along the mat and in another instant the whole sail was afire. The illumination lasted only a fraction of a minute, but while it burned the flames leaped twenty feet upward and threw a blinding glare on the nearer waves.

Jeff held his breath while the last red sparks fell hissing. It was darker than ever, now that the blaze had died. He rubbed his eyes and stared eastward but he could no longer make out the schooner's canvas.

Shivering, he crouched down on the wet logs to wait. If his flare had been seen it would take the schooner time to put about and sail two miles close-hauled. The wind was rising—coming over in brief, hard gusts. It rocked the raft and drenched the boy with spray. He tried to count off the minutes but his mind wandered stupidly. After what seemed at least an hour he pulled himself up by the mast and shouted with all the breath he could muster.

And to his unbelieving ears came an answering hail, loud and cheerful.

CHAPTER XVIII

THE FACE that leaned over Jeff's was thin, brown and smiling.

"Ah reckon yo'll come round in right smart of a hurry now, sonny," said a drawling southern voice. "Yo' was clean out o' yo' haid when we fetched yo' abo'd. How yo' feelin' now?"

"Better," Jeff answered weakly. "Where am I?"

He could feel the heave and strain of timbers

around him and see deck beams overhead.

"This yeah's the schooner *Currituck*," the man replied. "Privateer o' ten guns out of Edenton. Ah'm Cap'n Huber Wayne, at yo' service. Right now we're hove to—ridin' out the tail end of a storm."

"Yes," Jeff sighed. "The storm. Guess you picked me up just in the nick o' time, an' I sure thank you for it. The raft wouldn't have held together in a sea like this."

"How long yo' been floatin' round on it?" the Carolina skipper asked.

" 'Most a week. Say—" Jeff made an effort to sit up. "How long has the storm been blowing?"

"Most o' the night. But she's about finished now. Why?"

"I was wondering if we could figure the bearings of an island," Jeff explained. Slowly, with rests between sentences, he told his story. "The raft couldn't have drifted more'n two hundred miles," he concluded. "An' up to the last day it was all due west. Think you could find the place?"

Captain Wayne nodded thoughtfully. "We got to get yo' friend off, that's certain," he said. "Let's see—a high peak all by itself, two hundred miles eastward. Ah've never been there, but we'll sho' have a try at it. Think yo' could eat somethin' now?"

.   .   .   .

It was two days later that the lookout in the foretop sighted land. Jeff, almost himself again now, climbed the shrouds and saw the distant blue cone on the southeastern horizon.

"That's it!" he shouted. "Not above three hours' sail, with this wind!"

By that time he was familiar with every stick of the fast little schooner and the forty-odd members of her soft-spoken, hard-fighting crew. She had been commissioned only a month before and had already taken two enemy merchantmen as prizes. Watching the smart way they handled their vessel, he had come to have a high regard for the seamanship of these lazy-looking southerners.

By noon they were heading in for the break

in the barrier reef. Jeff stood by the helmsman to help pilot the schooner into the lagoon, but as soon as they were safely through he ran to the bows. There was no sign of Amos on the beach.

"He's probably seen us, sir, but he's scared we're British," Jeff told the captain. "Could we run up some colors?"

As the privateer came to anchor a bundle of red-white-and-blue bunting was hauled to the masthead. And hardly had the breeze shaken out the folds of the flag when a half-naked figure appeared, galloping madly down the beach.

"Ahoy, there!" Jeff yelled at the top of his lungs. "Amos—it's me—I'm coming ashore!"

He tumbled into the small-boat before it hit the water and seized the bow oar. Laughing at his impatience, the rest of the rowers laid to with a will and it was only a moment before the prow ran grating up the sand.

"Jeff!" the stocky young castaway quavered. "Durn if ye ain't back! I'd about g-g-give up hope of ever seein' ye again!"

They carried Amos back aboard for a meal

of hardtack and good North Carolina salt pork, and he was outfitted, as Jeff had been, with a reasonably whole shirt and breeches out of the slop-chest. After that another landing party was sent ashore for fresh fruit and coconuts. The two boys went with them.

"There's something we want to get before we sail," Jeff explained to the captain. "Maybe we can make it up to you for picking us up like you did."

Wayne laughed. "Yo' don't need to bother yo'self 'bout that, Jeff," he answered kindly. "Go 'long an' fetch yo' belongin's."

With the help of the *Currituck's* seamen they set up a proper marker on Jonas Beale's grave. Then the two lads made a last expedition to the cave. When they returned an hour later they were carrying the heavy box between them. The sailors laughed at their sweating faces. "Must be full o' dipsey leads," one of them guessed. "Let's heft it. Golly—she's heavy, sho' 'nough!"

That night in Wayne Huber's little cabin the boys opened the chest and showed him their dis-

THE TWO LADS MADE A LAST EXPEDITION
TO THE CAVE

covery. His jaw dropped when he saw the heap of gold and silver coins. But when they offered him a one-third share as a reward for their rescue he shook his head stubbornly.

"If yo' want to do somethin' fo' the crew, give 'em each one o' those big silver pieces," he said. "Ah'd call it a mighty handsome present, at that. But keep the rest. After what y'all have been through, yo've earned it!"

Jeff and Amos had taken their places as regular members of the schooner's crew and were assigned to the starboard watch. Through a week of good weather they cruised northward outside the French Islands, swung westerly to skirt Porto Rico and hove to off the Windward Passage. There they lay for three days watching the channel for a possible British sail.

On the first of November Captain Wayne decided there were no prizes coming out of Jamaica, and took advantage of a brisk breeze to head northwestward again among the low-lying islands of the Bahama group. They chased a small brig into Nassau, sheering off just before they came in range of the land guns, and proceeded north once more.

"Ah reckon you boys won't be sorry to see home," Wayne told Jeff. "We'll put in to rerig an' take on fresh provisions if the coast's clear, an' y'all can make the rest o' the trip overland."

As they moved up the Carolina shore a fishing-boat warned them that a British frigate was patrolling the approaches to Beaufort. For that reason the *Currituck* left Cape Lookout far to port and headed for Ocracoke Inlet.

Jeff and Amos were on deck that hazy morning when the dunes came into view. The schooner had an east wind abeam and was cutting along at a good eight knots. As she began to buck the tide-rips at the entrance of the inlet, Wayne told his first mate to call all hands. "Better clear fo' action," he said. "Might be a sloop-o'-war lyin' up behind the island."

But it was no sloop they saw, as they sailed through into Pamlico Sound. A bare mile to windward, her spars hidden until now by trees on the headland, rode a 38-gun frigate. Her lookout must have sighted the schooner's approach, for her topsails and courses were already set and the royals filled out even as they watched.

There was no time for the privateer to come about and claw back through the passage. "Ease the sheets an' put the helm over!" yelled the skipper. "We'll run fo' Marsh Point over yonder!"

As soon as they were before the wind the foresail was jibed and the schooner sped along like a bird with spread wings. But the maneuver was carried out none too soon. With all her canvas set the bigger ship was coming down fast in pursuit.

When he was no longer needed at the tackle, Jeff came aft and took his first good look at the frigate. "That's the *Albatross!*" he told Huber Wayne. "See that white patch in the foretopsail? She got a shot-hole there when we fought a Frenchman off Cape Finisterre. She's mighty fast before the wind, sir."

"Ah can see that." The Carolinian smiled grimly. "What's she carry fo' bow-chasers?"

"Two long twelves," Jeff answered. "I'd say she was within range now if she wanted to use 'em."

Within the next minute a shot came skipping by, a score of yards to starboard. Wayne spat contemptuously over the rail. "We can lay our little stern gun closer'n that," he said. "Come on, yere—Bell—Maxwell—man the six-pounder."

They rammed home a heavy charge of powder, lifted the swivel-gun's nose and were taking aim when the frigate's second ball screamed over. It was close above their heads. Jeff heard a rending crash as the shot took a splinter out of one side of the mainmast and plowed on through the fore-rigging.

Unperturbed, the gun crew let go with the six-pounder. It was an amazingly good shot. Even at that distance, they could see one of the frigate's jib-stays part and a torn headsail flutter to the deck.

"Won't be much mo' firin' till they've cleared that mess," the mate remarked with satisfaction. "Lively, for'ard there, an' get them shrouds spliced!"

For twenty miles across the open sound the chase continued. Try as they would, the *Currituck's* men could coax no more speed out of her, and the frigate was gaining, slowly but surely. After a breathing-spell of a few minutes her bow-guns took up the bombardment once more. Only one shot took effect, ripping a wide hole in the main topsail, but a number of others came too close for comfort.

Jeff flinched as a ball hit water a yard from the schooner's stern and threw spray above the bulwark. "If one o' those gets our steering-gear," he told Amos, "they'll have us in a tight spot. An' those gunners at the long twelves know it as well as we do."

Huber Wayne heard him and strolled nearer. "Yo' right, lad," he said. "We've been lucky so far. With a bit mo' lead we could have ducked in behind Cedar Island, but she's right on our heels."

He cast a thoughtful eye forward to the gray line of a long, sandy point, in sight over the port bow. "That *Albatross,* now," he remarked. "How much water yo' reckon she'll draw, Jeff?"

"I'd say she had to have four fathom, clear," the boy answered. "What do you think, Amos?"

"Easy four. She'd g-g-go aground at a half over three."

"Hmm," the captain mused. "An' two fathom is a plenty fo' us." He nodded and pursed his lips. "If yo' friends aren't too familiar with these waters," he said softly, "we-all might show 'em a trick."

He turned to the helmsman. "Keep her as she is," he ordered. "An' up for'ard, there—start the lead goin'."

"You mean there's a bar off the point?" Jeff asked eagerly.

"Right. It runs out a good two miles. There's less'n three fathom o' water over it at this tide, an' it shoals off so steep both sides, a ship moving fast would be right on it 'fore she knew. On a bright day yo' can tell it's there by the color o' the water—but with this haze—" he looked aloft, then grinned at the boys. "Anyhow," he finished, "if the frigate smells a rat an' changes course she's boun' to lose a few miles."

The leadsman in the bows was droning his soundings. "By the mark, ten . . . quarter less ten . . . by the mark, nine . . . and a half, nine."

Jeff looked southward at the point and saw that it was now almost abeam. For a moment he thought the captain must be mistaken. Nine fathoms was a lot of water here in the sound, and if the bar ran straight out they must be coming over it now.

Suddenly the cry of the leadsman changed. "A half, three!" he yelled. And after a quick cast, ". . . by the mark, three!"

The schooner surged across the shoal without slackening speed. Huber Wayne laughed as another round-shot skipped past. "Keep on a-shootin', there, British bulldogs!" he urged. "Yo' mighty nigh got us, now!" And he steadied his spyglass over the taffrail to watch the enemy's movements.

"They've got a lead goin' in the fore-chains,"

he announced after a moment. "But Ah do believe they're comin' straight on!"

Jeff could see that there was no sign of a
change of course aboard the frigate. Her yards
were still squared and she was plunging along
with a fine white bone in her teeth.

"Ready at the main sheet," the captain
ordered. "We'll jibe an' head south—give 'em
the idea we're runnin' up-river to New Bern!"

By the time the big boom had been put over
and the schooner was running with the wind on
her port beam, the pursuing ship was very close
to the bar. Jeff watched her, fascinated, his hands
clenched tight on the rail. He had a queer feeling
of pride in the frigate's beauty—a dread of seeing what was about to happen to her.

When it came it was far less of a spectacle
than he had imagined. At the last moment some
warning must have reached the big warship's
quarterdeck for there was a frantic hauling of
yards as she tried to come into the wind. It was
too late. They saw her spars shiver a little and
the foot of the foretopsail blew out as she

rammed, bow on, into the sand. Then with slow dignity she heeled over, her open deck canted at a steep angle.

"Ee-yah!" yelled Wayne. "Look at that! Every broadside gun out o' commission! An' there won't be enough tide to right her fo' two hours yet. Come on, boys—we're goin' about!"

In less than a minute the schooner had swung handily into the wind and was beating up to leeward of the bar. On the frigate a swarm of topmen were taking in sail as fast as the slant of the spars would let them. Perhaps they thought that without the pull of the wind she might right herself. If so, their hopes were vain. Even under bare poles she still lay like a log in the pounding waves.

The Carolina skipper was deadly calm now. "Ready at your guns, boys," he told the crew softly. "We're comin' in close—just short o' musket range. Point-blank it is, an' load with round shot. Hull her if yo' can."

Jeff was relieved to hear the order. Grape or chain-shot at that range would have meant sheer murder on the frigate's crowded deck. Wayne wanted to cripple the enemy vessel rather than to slaughter the crew.

With the Stars and Stripes whipping at her peak, the privateer bore down on her helpless victim. Waiting by the breech of his eighteen-pounder, Jeff wondered what Nate Winslow and the other Yankee seamen on the *Albatross* were thinking at that moment.

They had tacked so close now that he could almost recognize the grim faces of the marines, lined up along the lower rail.

"Sta'bo'd battery," came Captain Wayne's even voice, "fire as yo' bear!"

The guns began to thunder. Five reports, spaced a second or two apart. Then, as the smoke blew clear, a high-pitched yell broke from the schooner's crew. Five gaping, splintered holes showed the accuracy of their aim—three along the waterline, one where the bulwark met the deck and one right at the base of the foremast. A futile spray of musket-balls spattered the water without reaching the privateer.

"Look smart, there!" called Wayne. "Ready to bring her about!"

But even as he took his place at the main sheet, Jeff saw the figure of a man arch out in a long, clean dive from the frigate's forward deck.

"It's Nate Winslow!" he cried. "Look—he's trying to swim to us! Come on, Nate!"

CHAPTER XIX

THE SWIMMER drove through the water with long, thrashing strokes, making all the distance he could before the marines had time to reload their muskets. A few scattered balls spurted angrily in the water about him, but he drew steadily away from the ship.

"They've g-g-got a boat lowered!" yelled Amos. "They're comin' after him!"

"Port yo' helm," Wayne ordered. "Keep her

close to the wind an' we'll run in fo' him!"

Jeff had rushed to the bow gun and was helping ram home the cartridge and six-pounder ball. Over his shoulder he could see the frigate's cutter already overhauling his friend, the oars flashing at a furious beat.

The schooner had come smartly into the wind when the captain appeared at Jeff's side. "I can lay a gun," the boy panted. "Will you let me try one—for Nate?"

Wayne looked at his tense face and nodded. "Better take yo' time an' make it good," he said. "They'll have him sho' if yo' miss."

Jeff drew a long breath. It was point-blank range—no need to figure elevation. He swung the breech left—right—and eased the gun into position with the muzzle bearing square on the cutter's bow. A glance at the priming, another sight along the barrel, and he jerked the lanyard.

The gun barked and a cloud of acrid smoke blew back in the boy's face. As it cleared he saw the cutter jump in the water, the rowers tumbling forward like tenpins. Then the boat began to fill, going down rapidly by the head. Jeff saw his old enemy, Scallon, stand up in the stern-sheets waving his arms just before the craft swamped. And in a matter of seconds the whole crew was splashing and spluttering in the choppy waves.

The *Currituck* ran in till she was under the musket fire of the frigate and Amos stood ready in the bow-chains with a rope. As they surged closer they could see that the Yankee seaman's strength was nearly gone. He had been swimming at top speed for several minutes now, and his arms were heavy with weariness.

Amos threw the rope true and it splashed within a yard of the exhausted sailor's head. As he grasped it the *Currituck's* men gave a yell of triumph. It was the work of a moment to haul him over the side, and the schooner fell away gracefully, skimming out of range of the marines' vicious fire.

Jeff was the first to seize his friend's dripping hand. "You old son-of-a-gun!" he cried, and then checked himself. There was a stream of blood mingling with the sea water that dripped to the deck. "Gosh, Nate," the boy said, "you've been hit!"

The Maine man showed his teeth in a tired grin. "Tain't but a scratch," he gasped. "Creased my shoulder, I reckon."

A quick examination showed the wound was not serious. The musket-ball had torn a shallow furrow in the flesh of the shoulder muscle and a bandage soon stopped the bleeding.

Meanwhile another boat had put off from the *Albatross* and was picking up the cutter's crew. Huber Wayne watched them through his glass.

"None of 'em look to be drowned," he chuckled, "but they got right smart of a wettin'. That was a pretty shot, Jeff. It saved yo' friend's hide an' no foolin'."

He studied the frigate and considered. "Ah'd love to take her in fo' a prize," he said regretfully. "With another hundred men Ah'd bo'd her quick enough. Likely she'll be off the bar in a couple of hours, but we've got enough shot left to give her one mo' broadside."

At his order the schooner put about and tacked across the shoal to windward of the stranded enemy. The starboard guns were loaded and run out.

"Never mind her riggin'," the captain advised. "They can fix that quick enough, but she won't sail so lively with a few mo' holes in her hull."

Heeled over as she was, the frigate's starboard side showed a strip of copper sheathing below the waterline, and methodically the *Currituck's* gunners made it their target. When the guns stopped bellowing there were four more jagged holes to prove their accuracy.

"Sort of ashamed to do that," Wayne grinned. "Like shootin' a sittin' bird. Well, she'll do mighty little damage fo' the next few weeks."

As the schooner sailed northward from the scene of the battle, Jeff and Amos squatted beside Nate Winslow on the sunny fore deck and exchanged news. Nate's own story was briefly told. He had been locked up in the brig with the *Albatross* moored at the island for water—apparently because they suspected he might try to escape. Not till after the frigate was at sea again had he learned of his three countrymen's disappearance. For two months the British ship had been on patrol off the Virginia and North Carolina capes, but outside of capturing a few small snows and ketches she had seen little action.

"This mornin' they fergot to put me under hatches," he finished with a grin. "I tried to git them two Gloucester lads to come with me, but one was scairt an' t'other couldn't swim. I waited till the marines had let off their first volley an' took a runnin' dive. But what I want to know is, how'd ye make out on that island, an' what brung ye aboard here?"

As the boys unfolded their tale Nate whistled. "Sounds like ye'd done right well fer yerselves," he exclaimed. "Must be thousands o' dollars in that chest ye found. What ye aim to do with it?"

"We've talked about that," said Jeff. "Amos an' I thought maybe we'd try to buy a schooner an' fix her up, if we could find one cheap enough."

Nate looked pleased. "Jest what I'd hoped

ye'd say," he nodded. "I'd like to sail with ye if 'twarn't fer this war. But right now I want to git in a few licks at the cussed British."

"You mean you'll join the navy?"

"I might. Or one o' these fast privateers. That's where ye git action—an' prize money too."

By nightfall the schooner was fifty miles up Pamlico Sound, and when day dawned she was sailing through the pass behind Croatan Island.

"We'll take y'all up the Pasquotank an' set yo' off at Elizabeth City," Huber Wayne told his Yankee passengers. "If yo' goin' on to No'-folk, it's only a day's ride from there in the stage."

They had a farewell party that night at their moorings off the Carolina town. Amos made a stammering speech of thanks that delighted the *Currituck's* crew, and Jeff brought added cheers by passing out Spanish silver pieces to every man aboard.

At daybreak they shook hands with the captain and went ashore to take seats in the Norfolk

stage. The bare trees and the brown, bleak land-
scape startled Jeff at first. It was almost winter,
he realized—mid-November. Up in New England there might be snow on the ground now,
and folks would be getting ready for Thanks-
giving!

The journey took all day, jolting slowly over
the rough roads, and they were tired enough of
the musty-smelling coach before the roofs of
Norfolk came in sight at dusk.

"Why in tunket anybody'd want to travel this
way when they could go by sea," Nate grumbled,
"is past all understandin'."

They went to a chandler's shop by the wharves
that night and outfitted themselves in decent seamen's clothes before looking for lodgings. It was
late in the evening when they found a room at
Gobody's Tavern, close to the waterfront, and
all three of them were weary enough to sleep like
logs in their comfortable beds.

In the morning Nate volunteered to do a little
scouting among the seafaring men of the town.
"You an' Amos had best stay here," he told Jeff.

"That chest o' money is a durn sight too valuable to let out o' yer sight. I'll jest wander 'round a bit with my ears open. Might be a Yankee coaster in port that's plannin' to run the blockade. If we could git berths aboard her we'd be home by Christmas, likely."

After he had gone Jeff asked the landlord for paper and quills and sat down to write a letter to his father. It took him most of the morning, for the account of his adventures covered many pages.

"It may be," he wrote in conclusion, "that before this letter comes to Shinnequid, I will be there myself. However, I am told that the post is fairly certain as far as New York and doubtless beyond, as well. I would take great joy to think that you might even be reading these lines in as little time as three weeks, for I know that you must suppose me lost, or at best a prisoner in an enemy ship. Hoping for a speedy meeting with you, I remain, sir, r's'p'y yr. son, Jeffrey Robbins."

At Amos' request he added an enclosure to be

forwarded to Mrs. Gilman. "I never was no hand at writin'," the big lad blushed. "She couldn't m-m-make out to read my hen-scratches anyhow, an' if she jest knows I'm alive, I'll be satisfied."

The boys did justice to a dinner of good roast beef and potatoes, topped off with apple pie. Then Amos went upstairs to guard their money-chest, and Jeff put on his new peajacket and glazed hat. He would take a stroll in the town and post his letter, he decided. When he had left it with the clerk at the stage office and paid his two-shilling fee, he wandered on toward the docks. There was plentiful evidence of the effectiveness of the British blockade. Tall ships by the dozen were tied up along the wharfsides, their cordage sagging with disuse. Schooners and smaller craft were harder to find. Most of that class of vessels, he realized, were being put into service as privateers.

Jeff was approaching the inn an hour or so later, when he saw a man look up at the swinging sign and briskly cross the threshold ahead of him. As the boy walked through the parlor the stranger had already taken his seat at one of the tables and was calling for a tankard of ale.

There was something about the clipped, nasal speech that stopped Jeff in his tracks. He turned and took a closer look at the speaker. The man was thick-set, square-shouldered and square-jawed. He wasn't tall but he sat very erect in his neat blue watch-coat and there was a look of force and authority in his bearing. A pair of keen blue eyes looked out at the boy from under grizzled brows.

Jeff reddened. "Pardon, sir," he said, "but—I thought from your way of talking you might be from New England."

"Aye, lad, that I am," said the stranger. "Cap'n Ebenezer Doane o' the brig *Wanderer,* out o' Portland."

"Portland—in Maine?" Jeff cried delightedly. "Why, that's only a biscuit-toss from my home port—Shinnequid Cove!"

"Ye don't say!" The Yankee skipper rose swiftly and thrust out a hard brown hand, square like the rest of him. "Here, landlord," he called. "Another mug of ale for a Maine man!"

Jeff laughed. "I'm not thirsty," he said. "I'd mighty well like to hear the news from down our way, though."

"Same as the rest o' the coast," the captain told him. "No trade to speak of. Folks grumblin' about this danged war, but buildin' bonfires an' holdin' torchlight parades whenever there's a vict'ry. Ye should ha' seen Portland the night we got word of *Old Ironsides'* beatin' the *Guerrière!* An' 'twas the same story when Jones captured the *Frolic* in his sloop *Wasp.* The navy's been showin' the British how to fight, lad. An' there'll be more o' the same before this is over."

Jeff had only heard of the American successes that morning and was still aglow with pride at the record of Yankee gunnery and seamanship. But Captain Doane wanted to know how he came to be in Norfolk. He gave him the facts in bare outline with no mention of the treasure.

"What we're hoping for now," he finished, "is to find a ship to take us home. You couldn't use a few able hands aboard your brig, could you, Captain?"

Doane's rugged face clouded for a moment. "Nothin' I'd like better," he said. "Fact is I put in here to refit. The *Wanderer's* a fast sailer—Bath-built, an' as sweet lines as ye'll see in a long day. Figgered I'd brace her ribs an' deck, get more height to her topmasts an' ship some guns fer a bit o' privateerin'. But there's no money left in the town. Hard cash is scarce anyhow, an' folks have invested all they had in Virginia privateers. Looks like I'm stranded here till I can raise the cost o' the job."

Jeff jerked his chair closer to the table. "You mean," he said, his eyes alight, "that you're looking for somebody to put money into the brig—on shares?"

"That's the size of it," the New Englander nodded briskly. "Why? Have ye any friends that would risk a few thousands in such a venture?"

Before Jeff could answer the door opened and Nate Winslow came stamping in out of the cold.

"Well, lad," he hailed Jeff cheerfully, "I believe I'm on the track o' somethin'."

He paused as he caught sight of the boy's companion. "Well, I'll be a goggle-eyed scrod!" he cried. "Cap'n Doane, ye're a sight to make a Maine man glad!"

The gray-haired skipper was on his feet, staring in his turn. "Why, Nate—ye long-legged swab!" he laughed. "It's been a dog's age since we sailed together."

They gripped each other's hands boisterously. "Come here to the table, man," the captain urged. "We'll drink to old times in the *Marianna!*"

Jeff did not try to interrupt the reunion, but sat listening and thinking. Doane, he learned, had been mate of the ship in which Nate had made his first voyages as a 'prentice seaman, nearly a dozen years before. He could see the regard his friend had for the older man, and it was not long before Nate was launched on a series of yarns that made the boy's blood tingle. The lanky sailor, who usually had so little to say, became almost voluble when he described Doane's feats of daring and seamanship.

"Here, that's enough o' such tales!" the captain growled. "I mind there was times I was glad to have ye at my back, too—green hand as ye were—but I reckon our young friend here has heard more'n he can stomach already. I never knew you was one to let yer tongue run on so, Nate."

The big seaman grinned. "I don't often git a feller like Ebenezer Doane to talk about," he answered. "But, say—what I started to tell Jeff when I came in was that I sighted a handsome little Yankee brig moored in the channel. Know anything about her, Cap'n? They tell me she's called the *Wanderer*."

CHAPTER XX

CAPTAIN DOANE winked at Jeff. "I cal'late I might give ye some information, if I was pressed," he said. "I own that *Wanderer* brig, myself."

Jeff could control himself no longer. "Wait," he told Nate excitedly. "Don't ask another question till I've brought Amos down. What I've got to say is his business too, long as he's my partner."

He dashed up the stairs, his new clogs pounding on the worn oak. Amos, faithfully guarding the treasure, was reproachful when he burst in.

"Where'd ye go?" he asked. "I been c-c-cooped up here all afternoon, seems like—"

"Come on!" Jeff interrupted. "You'll hear some real news down in the parlor." He shoved the chest, wrapped in old sailcloth and tied with ropes, farther under the bed. "That'll be safe," he said, and led the way downstairs.

When Amos had been introduced to Captain Doane, the four of them pulled their chairs up to the table. Jeff considered a moment, choosing his words.

"I think maybe this meeting was luckier for all of us than you can guess, Cap'n Doane," he said. "You've got a ship, and you're looking for money to fit her out as a privateer. Nate's looking for an officer's berth in just such a ship. And as for Amos and me—well, maybe we don't look it, but we've got money. All you need. Is that right, Nate?"

"Right as a trivet!" Nate grinned.

The skipper sat back and regarded each of them in turn, the sea-crinkles at the corners of his sharp eyes deepening into a smile. He slapped his thigh.

"Well, by thunder!" he exclaimed softly. "If that don't beat all! Looks like we ought to be able to make a deal, an' everybody be satisfied. Only thing is," he frowned, "it may take five or six thousand dollars to do the job right, an' I've only got about a thousand o' my own."

"The boys can lay their hands on a lot more'n that, Cap'n," Nate reassured him. "All you got to do is figger out the shares."

Before the candles were lighted the whole transaction was settled. Jeff and Amos would become the owners of a third interest in the brig, agreeing to pay the cost of her refitting, up to $5,000. Nate, happy as a clam at high water, was shipped as first mate and carried his dunnage aboard at once.

At the captain's suggestion, the boys took their money to the local bank next morning for safekeeping during their stay in Norfolk. Then, before they signed the necessary papers, they were rowed out to the *Wanderer*.

Doane's face glowed with honest pride as he showed them over the brig. "I watched her a-buildin'," he said, "and never did a sweeter ship come out o' Maine. Look at the oak in those timbers. There's not a weak joint in her hull nor a bad splice in her riggin'. But shucks—don't take my word for it. Look fer yerselves."

Everything the two lads saw increased their satisfaction. There was speed in the little ship's lines and staunchness too. Her deck planking gleamed and her tarry rigging was taut and new. She was small enough to handle easily in any weather, but big enough to mount eight or nine long guns on a side and carry a crew of a hundred fighting men.

"She's everything you say, Cap'n," Jeff laughed when they had finished their inspection. "We're ready to go before the notary right now, and the quicker we get to work on her the better we'll be pleased."

.   .   .   .

It was just thirty days later when the armed brig *Wanderer* rounded Shinnequid Head and ran smartly in with her yards trimmed to the quartering breeze.

Jeff, standing in the fore shrouds, drew in a deep breath of winter air laden with the smell of the salt marsh. Along the point the bayberry ledges lay deep under a blanket of white, but the waves that danced up the cove were the sapphire blue that he remembered.

The voyage up the coast had been easy enough. With half a dozen hands from the brig's former crew and an equal number signed on in Norfolk they had found no difficulty in handling sail. It was Captain Doane's idea, heartily endorsed by his young partners, that the regular crew of the *Wanderer* should be recruited in Maine.

After one brush with a British cruiser outside the Virginia Capes, it was clear that the brig could outfoot her enemies on any point of sailing. They had given New York a wide berth and crossed the mouth of Massachusetts Bay by night, so that no other hostile sail was sighted on the trip.

The waves chuckled merrily under the brig's forefoot, and with the tide to help her she was soon approaching the head of the little bay.

"Thar's the town!" yelled Amos from his perch in the cross-trees. "I can see the steeple— an' Deacon Neal's red barn!"

He scrambled down and joined Jeff at the braces, as Nate Winslow called the hands to heave to. Even while they were letting go the anchor they could see a crowd of townspeople running down to the wharf. Twenty minutes later the boys were in the brig's longboat, pulling for the shore.

Hardly had they reached the dock when the church bell began to ring wildly. Jeff interrupted a flood of questions to point anxiously toward the town. "What's the bell ringing for?" he asked. "Must be a fire!"

"No, it ain't, Jeff," a small boy answered with glee. "We seen yer faces when ye was in the boat an' the sexton's ringin' to let folks know ye're home!"

Their progress up the hill was slow. The crowd pressed about them, laughing, chattering, shaking their hands. At last Jeff was able to break through and reach the tavern stable, where he hired a horse and sleigh. With Amos beside him he drove off up the main street to the tune of cheers and jingling bells.

The Gilmans lived close to town, just beyond the schoolhouse. He left Amos there and went on alone, jogging down the three-mile stretch of narrow road that led to Tombstone Point. As the horse pulled over a rise Jeff had a view all the way down the point to the lonely tower of the lighthouse. He could see the reef and the flashes of white where the seas broke over it. And nearer but still distant, he could see a solitary man trudging toward him through the snow.

Eagerly the boy plied the whip. There was something familiar about that approaching fig-ure. "Hello-o, Dad!" he yelled at the top of his lungs and the startled horse broke into a run. The man in the road stood still, waiting, as if he doubted the evidence of his ears. But as Jeff drew nearer he saw the broad shoulders square themselves and the bearded face light up with love and pride.

"Jeff, boy," his father said huskily, "I'll believe it now. You're really home!"

There was a lot for them to tell each other as they drove on to the little house at the end of the point. Mr. Robbins had received Jeff's letter the week before. It had been glad news indeed, for the crew of the *Abigail* had long since been given up for lost.

"When I saw the brig come in, an' heard the church bells," said the older man, "I had a hope it might be you, so I started for town fast as I could."

Jeff spent all that afternoon with his father, and the winter dusk was falling when he drove back to Shinnequid. Candles made a soft, yellow light in farmhouse windows along the road. As he passed the school he heard a faint sound of singing, and knew the children must be practicing Christmas carols inside.

He swung into the main street and his heart began to beat faster. Patience Deering had not been in the crowd at the wharf, but he had learned from his father that she was expected home that day from the young ladies' school in Portsmouth, where she was finishing her education.

There were lights shining out on the snow from the windows of the big house. He tied the horse to the hitching post, marched up the walk to the door and thumped the knocker boldly. While he waited, staring at the fine paneling and the lovely fanlight above the doorway, he had a feeling of humility. This was a house for gracious living. The girl who had grown up in it was a lady, gently born and reared. And though a rough sailorman like himself might become her equal in wealth, it behooved him to become a gentleman as well. In free America even that was possible. Almost fiercely he promised himself that when this war was over he would try for admission to Bowdoin College. There he would get an education that no man need be ashamed of.

In the midst of these turbulent thoughts the door was opened and a servant showed him into the hall. "The squire's in the library," the woman told him. "I'll let Miss Patience know you're here."

The boy felt all his confidence ooze out of him as he stepped into the presence of Squire Deering. The magistrate was a big man. Even sitting down he had an air of importance. Gold seals gleamed on the ponderous watch chain that stretched across his rounded waistcoat. But as he laid down his book and peered judicially at Jeff over his spectacles, there was a twinkle of humor in his shrewd eyes.

"Hm-m!" he rumbled. "You're the Robbins boy I've heard about. Yes, yes. Sit down, young man. Calling on my daughter, eh?"

Jeff bowed slightly. "Yes, sir," he replied.

The squire's eyebrows lifted quizzically as he studied the lad before him. "Hm-m!" he said again. "You aren't dressed like any dandy, it's sure. And yet I heard you'd come into a fortune of some sort. Is that a fact?"

"When Amos Gilman and I were marooned in the West Indies," Jeff answered, "we found a chest full of old Spanish money. In Norfolk we got it changed for United States currency—'round twenty-six thousand dollars, it came to."

"And half o' that's yours?"

"I've left ten thousand dollars in the bank. The rest we put into that brig in the harbor. Amos and I own a third share between us, and soon as we've shipped a crew we're going to take some British prizes."

The boy had spoken a bit defiantly at first, but now he felt more at ease. "When I come home again," he said, "there's something I'll be wanting to talk to you about, sir."

He could feel his face reddening as he waited for the older man to speak, but there was no answer except a subdued chuckle. Then came a patter of feet on the stairs and Patience appeared in the doorway. For a moment he hardly knew her. She was taller—lovelier—a woman in dress and manner. But there was no disguising the warmth that shone in her eyes.

"Oh, *Jeff!*" she cried softly. "I'm so glad to see you!" And as he stepped forward to meet her, her two hands fell naturally into his.

"Squire Deering, sir," said Jeff, "do you mind if I ask your daughter to take a little sleigh-ride? I'll bring her back in time for supper."

Patience laughed. "Of course he doesn't mind! Wait for me in the hall, Jeff." And with a swirl of skirts she was away up the stairs.

They drove out the cove road in the direction of Shinnequid Head. It was a still evening, cold but clear, and the stars sparkled like points of white fire overhead.

"There's the *Wanderer*." Jeff pointed toward the dark shape floating in the middle of the chan-nel. "You must see her tomorrow—come aboard, I mean, and really see her. Oh, but she's a beauty, Patience! And guns enough to tackle anything short of a frigate, lone-handed. With any luck we'll make a fortune out of her."

They had driven to the end of the road and turned homeward once more when he finished the tale of his adventures. Then they were silent for a while, warm under the bearskin robe, looking out at the snow and the stars.

"Patience," Jeff said abruptly, "there's something I brought you. We'll be sailing in a week or two, if the recruiting goes well, and maybe I won't see Shinnequid again for a couple of years. I thought I'd—like to know you had these—"

He took off his mitten and fumbled inside his coat, pulling out a tiny leather pouch. Patience looked at him questioningly and untied the drawstring. As she opened the pouch, six great white pearls cascaded into her hand, gleaming in the starlight.

"Oh, Jeff—they're *beautiful!*" she whispered. "And I'll be ever so proud to keep them for you."

"For me? No—that's not what I meant," he stammered. "They belong to you, Patience. Only—well, it may be a long time, and—"

"Yes," she told him quietly. "I understand. I'll wait, Jeff."

www.ingramcontent.com/pod-product-compliance
Lightning Source LLC
Chambersburg PA
CBHW030558170726

48283CB00002B/385